# MARS IS MY DESTINATION

By
FRANK BELKNAP LONG

I0541540

ARMCHAIR FICTION
PO Box 4369, Medford, Oregon 97504

*For more information about Armchair Books and products, visit our
website at…*

**www.armchairfiction.com**

*Or email us at…*

**armchairfiction@yahoo.com**

# MARS...

*Earth's first colony in Space. Men killed for the coveted ticket that allowed them to go there. And, once there, the killing went on...*

# MARS...

*Ralph Graham's goal since boyhood—and he was Mars-bound with authority that put the whole planet in his pocket—if he could live long enough to assert it!*

# MARS...

*Source of incalculable wealth for humanity and deadly danger for those who tried to get it!*

# MARS...

*In Earth's night sky, a symbol of the god of war—in this tense novel of the future, a vivid setting for stirring action!*

# CAST OF CHARACTERS

### RALPH GRAHAM
*He was brought in to resolve a major conflict within the Martian Colony—and it might cost him his life.*

### COMMANDER LITTLEFIELD
*Having to deal with all the small emergencies on a sky ship was one planet-sized headache!*

### JOHN LYNTON
*Talk about bringing your work home with you… what better place to hide six nuclear fuel cylinders!*

### JOSEPH SHERWOOD
*The push of a button could vaporize the entire Colony— and he had the power to push it.*

### HENRY WENDEL
*He loved his job—and it required him to resort to brutal violence two or three times a week.*

### HELEN BARCLAY
*Beautiful but deadly. She did something no one had ever done before—stowed away on a Mars ship.*

### JOAN GRAHAM
*She wouldn't go to Mars with him—tomorrow or ever. She was loving and boring as the day is long.*

# CHAPTER ONE

I'D KNOWN FOR TEN MINUTES THAT something terrible was going to happen. It was in the cards, building to a zero-count climax.

The spaceport bar was filled with a fresh, washed-clean smell, as if all the winds of space had been blowing through it. There was an autumn tang in the air as well, because it was open at both ends, and out beyond was New Chicago, with its parks and tall buildings, and the big inland sea that was Lake Michigan.

It was all right...if you just let your mind dwell on what was outside. Men and women with their shoulders held straight and a new lift to the way they felt and thought, because Earth wasn't a closed circuit any more. Kids in the parks pretending they were spacemen, bundled up in insulated jackets, having the time of their lives. A blue jay perched on a tree, the leaves turning red and yellow around it. A nurse in a starched white uniform pushing a perambulator, her red-geld hair whipped by the wind, a dreamy look in her eyes.

Nothing could spoil any part of that. It was there to stay and I breathed in deeply a couple of times, refusing to remember that in the turbulent, round-the-clock world of the spaceports Death was an inveterate barhopper.

Then I did remember, because I had to. You can't bury your head in the sand to shut out ugliness for long, unless you're ostrich-minded and are willing to let your integrity go down the drain.

I didn't know what time it was and I didn't much care. I only knew that Death had come in late in the afternoon, and was hovering in stony silence at the far end of the bar.

He was there, all right, even if he had the same refractive index as the air around him and you could see right through him. The sixth-sense kind of awareness that everyone experiences at times—call it a premonition, if you wish—had started an alarm bell ringing in my mind.

It was still ringing when I raised my eyes, and knew for sure that all the furies that ever were had picked that particular time and place to hold open house.

I saw it begin to happen.

It began so suddenly it had the impact of a big, hard-knuckled fist crashing down on the spaceport bar, startling everyone, jolting even the solitary drinkers out of their private nightmares.

Actually the violence hadn't quite reached that stage. But it was a safe bet that it would in another ten or twelve seconds. And when it did there was no chain or big double lock on Earth that could keep it from terminating in bloodshed.

The tip-off was the way it started, as if a fuse had been lit that would blow the place apart. Just two voices for an instant, raised in anger, one ringing out like a pistol shot. But I knew that something was dangerously wrong the instant I caught sight of the two men who were doing the arguing.

The one whose voice had made every glass on the long bar vibrate like a tuning fork was a blond giant, six-foot-four at least and built massive around the shoulders. His shirt was open at the throat and his chest was sweat-sheened and he had the kind of outsized ruggedness that made you feel it would have taken a heavy rock-crushing machine a full half-hour to flatten him out.

The other was of average height and only looked small by contrast. He was more than holding his own, however, standing up to the Viking character defiantly. His weather-beaten face was as tight as a drum, and his hair was standing straight up, as though a charge of high-voltage electricity had passed right through him.

He just happened to have unusually bristly hair, I guess. But it gave him a very weird look indeed.

I don't know why someone picked that critical moment to shout a warning, because everyone could see it was the kind of argument that couldn't be stopped by anything short of strong-armed intervention. Advice at that point could be just as dangerous as pouring kerosene on the fuse, to make it burn faster.

But someone did yell out, at the top of his lungs. "Pipe down, you two! What do you think this is, a debating society?"

It could have turned into that, all right, the deadliest kind of debating society, with the stoned contingent taking sides for no sane reason. It could have started off as a free-for-all and ended with five or six of the heaviest drinkers lying prone, with bashed-in skulls.

The barkeep made a makeshift megaphone of his two hands and added to the confusion by shouting: "Get back in line or I'll have you run right out of here. I'll show you just how tough I can get. Every time something like this happens I get blamed for it. I'm goddam sick of being in the middle."

"That's telling them, John! Need any help?"

"No, stay where you are. I can handle it."

I didn't think he could, not even if he was split down the middle into two men twice his size. I didn't think anyone could, because by this time I'd had a chance to take a long, steady, camera-eye look at the expression on the Viking character's face.

I'd seen that expression before and I knew what it meant. The Viking character was having a virulent sour grapes reaction to something Average Size had said. It had really taken hold, like a smallpox vaccination that's much too strong, and his inner torment had become just agonizing enough to send him into a towering rage.

Average Size had probably been boasting, telling everyone how lucky he was to be on the passenger list of the next Mars-bound rocket. And in a crowded spaceport bar, where Martian Colonization Board clearances are at a terrific premium, you don't indulge in that kind of talk. Not unless you have a suicide complex and are dead set on leaving the earth without traveling out into space at all.

Now things were coming to a head so fast there was no time to cheat Death of his cue. He was starting to come right out into the open, scythe swinging, punctual to the dot. I was sure of it the instant I saw the gun gleaming in the Viking character's hand and the smaller man recoiling from him, his eyes fastened on the weapon in stark terror.

*Oh, you fool!* I thought. *Why did you provoke him? You should have expected this, you should have known. What good is a Mars clearance if you end up with a bullet in your spine?*

For some strange reason the Viking character seemed in no hurry to blast. He seemed to be savoring the look of terror in Average Size's eyes, letting his fury diminish by just a little, as if by allowing a tenth of it to escape through a steam-spigot safety valve he could make more sure of his aim. It made me wonder if I couldn't still get to them in time.

The instant I realized there was still a chance I knew I'd have to try. I was in good physical trim and no man is an island when the sands are running out. I didn't want to die, but neither did Average Size and there are obligations you can't sidestep if you want to go on living with yourself.

I moved out from where I was standing and headed straight for the Viking character, keeping parallel with the long bar. I can't recall ever having moved more rapidly, and I was well past the barkeep—he was blinking and standing motionless, as white as a sheet now—when the Viking character's voice rang out for the second time.

"You think you're better than the rest of us, don't you? Sure you do. Why deny it? Who are you, who is anybody, to come in here and strut and put on airs? I'm going to let you have it, right now!"

The blast came then, sudden, deafening. They were standing so close to each other I thought for a minute the gun had misfired, for Average Size didn't stiffen or sag or change his position in any way and his face was hidden by smoke from the blast.

I should have known better, for it was a big gun with a heavy charge, and when a man is half blown apart his body can become galvanized for an instant, just as if he hasn't been hit at all. Sometimes he'll be lifted up and hurled back twenty feet and sometimes he'll just stand rigid, with the life going out of him in a rush, an instant before his knees give way and there's a terrible, welling redness to make you realize how mistaken you were about the shot going wild.

The smoke thinned out fast enough, eddying away from him in little spirals. But one quick look at him sinking down, passing into eternity with his head lolling, was all I had time for. Pandemonium was breaking loose all around me, and my only thought was to make a mad dog killer pay for what he had done before someone got between us.

Mad dog killers enrage me beyond all reason. Given enough provocation almost any man can go berserk and commit murder. But the Viking character had let a provocation that merited no more than a rebuke rip his self-control to shreds.

The naked brutality of it sickened me. Something primitive and very dangerous—or perhaps it was something super-civilized—made me out to beat him into insensibility before he could kill again. I felt like a man confronting a poisonous snake, who knows he must stamp on it or blast off its head before it can sink its fangs in his flesh.

I was not alone in feeling that way. All around me there was an angry muttering, a cursing and a shouting. If I needed support, sturdy backing, I had it. But right at that moment I didn't need it. An angry giant had come to life inside of me and we exchanged nods and understood each other.

There was a crash behind me, but I ignored it. What was harder to ignore was the barkeep straddling the bar and coming down flatfooted in the wake of two reeling drunks who were lunging for the killer with a crazy, wild look in their eyes. I didn't want them to get to him ahead of me.

He hadn't moved at all and had a frightened look on his face, as if the blast had jolted some sanity back into him and made him realize that you can't gun a man down in a crowded bar without adjusting a noose to your own throat and giving fifty men a chance to draw it tight.

The gun he'd killed with might still have saved him, if he'd swung about and started shooting up the bar. But I didn't give him a chance to recover.

I ploughed into him, wrenched the gun from him and sent him reeling back against the bar with a solidly delivered blow to the jaw, luckily aimed just right.

Then they were on him, five or six of them, and I couldn't see him for a moment.

I held the gun tightly and looked at it. It was still warm and just the feel of it sent a shiver up my spine. A gun that has just been wrenched from the hand of a killer is unlike any other weapon. There's blood on it, even if no laboratory test can bring it out.

I didn't know I'd lost anything until I looked down and saw my wallet lying on the floor at my feet. The energy I'd put into the blow had not only sent a stab of pain up my wrist to my elbow. It had jarred something loose from my inner breast pocket that had a danger-potential, right at that moment, which could have turned the tide of rage that was sweeping the bar away from the killer and straight in my direction. Some of it anyway, splitting it down the middle, causing the drunks who were divided in their minds about what he had done to change sides abruptly.

In my wallet was a perforated card, all stippled with tiny dots down one side, and it said that I was on the passenger list of the next Mars-bound rocket, and that the Martian Colonization Board clearance was of a peculiar kind…very special.

The wallet had fallen open and the card was in plain view for anyone to read. It could be recognized by its color alone—a light shade of blue—and if anyone who felt the way the killer had done about Average Size had caught sight of it and made a grab for the wallet—

I was bending to pick it up when a voice whispered close to my ear. "Don't let anyone see that card—if you want to stay in one piece. You'd better get out of here before they start asking questions. They won't wait for the Spaceport Police to get here. Too many of them will be in trouble if they don't find out fast where everyone stands. They'll know how to go about it."

I couldn't believe it for a minute, because I hadn't seen her come in. I'd noticed two women at the bar, but not this one—it would have been impossible for me to have failed to notice so slim a waist or hips so enchantingly rounded, or the honey-blonde hair piled high, or the wide, dark-lashed eyes that were staring at me out of a face that would have made a good many men with their lives at stake forget the meaning of danger.

Even if she'd been wedged in tightly between two male escorts at the bar, I'd have noticed a part of all that. Just one glimpse of the back of her head, with the indefinable, special quality that makes beauty like that perceptible at a glance, so that you know what the whole woman will look like when she turns, would have made so deep an impression on me that not even the violence I'd participated in a moment afterwards could have blotted it from my mind.

It left me speechless for an instant. I just snatched up the wallet, put it safely back in my pocket and returned her stare in complete silence.

"Better keep the gun," she advised. "Your fingerprints are all over it now. You could clear yourself all right, considering who you are. But it would be much simpler just to toss it into Lake Michigan, especially if they decide to let him go and lie about who did the killing."

I could have wiped the gun clean and tossed it on the floor, but I knew what was in her mind. You just don't leave a murder weapon lying around in plain view when you've picked it up right after a killing. It can lead to all kinds of complications.

I nodded and stood up. "Thanks for the advice," I said, finding my voice at last. "There are enough eye-witnesses here to convict him without this, if just a few of them have a conscience."

"Don't count on it," she said. "They're angry enough to kill him right now, because they don't like to see anyone gunned down like that. But when they've had time to think it over—"

She was right, of course. There were six or seven men struggling with the killer now but there were others who weren't. A fight had started near the middle of the bar and someone was shouting: "The ugly son deserved what he got! Every man who gets a Mars clearance now has to play along with the Colonization Board! He has to turn informer and help them set a trap for anyone who gets in their way. Just depriving us of our rights doesn't satisfy them. They're scheming to get the whole Mars Colony for themselves."

It was the Big Lie—the charge that had done more damage to the Mars Colony than the shortages of food and desperately needed construction materials, and almost as much damage as the two major power conflicts and the transportation difficulties that never seemed to get solved.

I wanted to go right up to him and grab hold of him and hit him as hard as I'd hit the Viking character, because he was a killer too—a killer of the dream.

But the blonde who seemed to know all the answers and what was wise and sane and sensible was tugging at my arm and I couldn't ignore the urgency in her voice.

"Time's running out on you, Mr. Important Man. If they find out just who you are, you won't have a chance of getting out of here alive. Every one of them will be clamoring for your blood. The pity of it, the terrible pity, is that most of them hate violence as much as you do. They hate what that wild beast just did. But the Big Lie has made them hate the Colonization Board even more. Do we go?"

It came as a surprise that she was leaving with me, and that was downright idiotic, in a way. With the place in an uproar, a killer still trying to break loose and a fight under way it would have been madness for her to stay, and the two other women had vanished without stopping to talk to anyone. But in moments of stress you can overlook the obvious and wonder about it afterward.

We had to move fast and we ran into trouble when two struggling drunks got in our way. I shouldered one aside and rammed an elbow into the stomach of the other and we reached the street without being stopped by anyone who didn't want us to leave. The card was back in my pocket and not a single one of them had X-ray eyes.

In another minute or two someone would have probably remembered that I'd disarmed the Viking character and could have had a reason for the fast violent way I'd gone about it. Then I'd have been in for the kind of questioning the blonde had mentioned—a kangaroo court interrogation before the Spaceport Police could get there. And if my answers had failed to satisfy them they would have wasted no time in turning my pockets inside out.

I'd been spared all that, thanks to that same blonde. And—I didn't even know her name!

## CHAPTER TWO

WE'D BEEN TALKING FOR TWENTY minutes and I still didn't know her name. She wasn't being secretive or coy or holding out on me because she didn't trust me as much as I trusted her. I just hadn't gotten around to asking her, because we were both still talking about what had happened at the bar and it was so closely tied in with what was happening in New York and London and Paris and every big city on Earth—and on Mars as well—that it dwarfed our puny selves—extra-special as the blonde's puny self happened to be from the male point of view.

I didn't know whether she was Helen or Barbara, Anne or Ruth or Tanya. I just knew that she was beautiful and that we were sipping Martinis and looking out through a wide picture window at New Chicago's lakeshore parklands enveloped in a twilight glow.

The restaurant was called the Blue Mandarin and it conformed in all respects to the picture that name conjures up—a diaphanous blue, oriental-ornate eating establishment with nothing to offer its patrons that was new, original, exciting, unique.

But there it was and there it would remain—until Lake Michigan froze solid. For the moment its artificial decor wasn't important to either of us. Only the Big Lie and what it was doing to the Martian Colonization Project.

"My father was one of the first," she said. "Do you know what it means, to stand in an empty, desolate waste, forty million miles from home, and realize you're one of the chosen few—that a city will some day grow from the seeds you've planted and nourished with your life blood?"

"I think I do," I said. "I hope I do."

"He died," she said, "when he was thirty years old, from a Martian virus they hadn't discovered how to combat until two-thirds of the first two thousand colonists succumbed to it."

"Why didn't he take you with him?" I asked. "There were no passenger restrictions then. The Colonization Board had great difficulty in finding enough volunteers."

"My mother refused to go," she said. "I'm afraid...most women are more conservative than men. Father died alone, and five years later Mother married a man who didn't want to be one of the first ten thousand—or the first sixty thousand. He had no problem. He wasn't like the men we saw tonight."

"If every man and woman on Earth wanted to go to Mars," I said, "the Colonization Board would have no problem. A demand on so colossal a scale could not be met—in a century and a half. And laws would be passed to prevent the scheming that's taking place everywhere, the hatred and the violence. The Big Lie would not be believed."

"I know," she said. "It's when only twenty thousand can go and five million want to go that you have a problem. A little hope filters through, and the five million become envious and enraged."

I looked at her. I was feeling the glow now, the warmth creeping through the cells of my brain, the recklessness that alcohol can generate in a man with a worry that looms as big as the Big Lie, to the part of himself that isn't dedicated to combating the Lie. The ego-centered, demandingly human part, the woman-needing part, the old Adam that's in all of us.

And suddenly I found myself thinking of Paris in the Spring, and the sparkling Burgundies of France and vineyards in the dawn and what it had meant to have a woman always at my side—or almost always—and in my bed as well.

New York, flag-draped for Autumn, London in a swirling fog, the old houses, the dreaming spires, anywhere on the round green Earth where there was laughter and music and a woman to share it with…

All that had been mine for ten years. But now, like a fool, I wanted Mars as well. Mars was in my blood and I could no longer rest content with what I had.

Take it with me to Mars? And why not? It was no problem…when you didn't have my problem. A quite simple problem, really. The woman I'd married wouldn't go with me to Mars.

She seemed to sense that I was having some kind of inward struggle, and was feeling a decided glow at the same time, for she reached out suddenly and took firm hold of my hand.

"Something's troubling you," she said. "Why don't you tell me about it while you're feeling mellow. Considering the kind of world we're living in, mellow is the best way to feel. It wears off quickly enough and next day you pay for it. But while it lasts, I believe in making the most of it. Don't you?"

Should I tell her, dared I? I might have to pay for it with a vengeance, for she'd probably think me quite mad. And I still had some old-fashioned ideas about loyalty and happened to be in love with my wife.

It was crazy, it made no sense, but that's the way it was. I looked at the woman sitting opposite me and wondered how a man could be in love with one woman and find another so attractive that he'd been on the verge of coming right out and asking her if she'd go with him to Mars.

I looked at her blonde hair piled up high, and her pale beautiful face and wondered how it would be if I hadn't been married to Joan at all.

I shut my eyes for a moment, thinking back, remembering the quarrel I'd had with my wife that morning, the quarrel I'd tried my best to forget over four straight whiskies at the spaceport bar late in the afternoon.

It was almost as if it was taking place again, right there at the table, with another woman sitting opposite me who could not hear Joan's angry voice at all.

"I mean every word I'm saying, Ralph Graham. You either tell them you're staying right here in New Chicago or I'm divorcing you. I won't go to Mars with you—tomorrow or next year or five years from now. Is that plain?"

It was plain enough. To cushion the shock of it, and ease the pain a little I stared into the fireplace, seeing for an instant in the high-leaping flames a red desert landscape and a city that towered to the brittle stars…white, resplendent, swimming in a light that never was on sea or land.

All right, the first Earth colony on Mars wasn't that kind of a city. It was rugged and sprawling and rowdy. It was filled with tumult and shouting, its prefabricated metal dwellings scoured and pitted by the harsh desert winds. But I liked it better that way.

I wanted to walk its crooked streets, to rejoice with its builders and creators, to be one of the first sixty thousand. With my mind and heart and blood and guts I wanted to be there before the cautious, solemn, over-serious people ruined it for the kind of man I was.

"I mean it, Ralph," Joan said. "If you go—you'll go alone. All of my friends are here, all of my roots. I won't tear myself up by the roots even for you. Much as I love you, I just won't."

It was five in the morning, and we'd been arguing half the night. In two more hours daylight would come flooding into the apartment again, and I'd probably have the worst talk-marathon hangover of my life.

I suddenly decided to go out into the cool dawn without saying another word to her, slamming the door after me to make sure she'd realize just how angry she'd made me.

I wouldn't even switch on the five A.M. news telecast or stop to take in the cat on my way out. Women and cats had a great deal in common, I told myself bitterly. They were arbitrary and stubborn and mysteriously intent on having their own way and keeping you guessing as to their real motives.

By heaven…if I had to go alone to Mars I'd go.

So I'd really hung one on, had gone out and made a round of the lakeside bars. All morning until noon and then I'd sobered up over coffee and a sandwich and started out again early in the afternoon. It just goes to show what a quarrel like that can do to a man's nerves and peace of mind and all of his plans for the future, for I'm not even a moderately heavy drinker.

Early morning bar traveling is barbarous, a lunatic-fringe pastime, and it was the first time in my life I'd resorted to it. But resort to it I did, and as the day wore on I gravitated from the lakeside taverns toward the spaceport in slow stages, and twice in five hours reached the stage where I couldn't have passed the straight-line test. If I hadn't sobered up a little at noon I'd have reached the big, dangerous bar as high as a man can get without falling flat on his face.

The Colonization Board hadn't even tried to stop what goes on there around the clock, because there are explosive tensions and hard to uncover areas of criminality in a city as big as New Chicago it's wise to provide a safety valve for—when Mars fever is running so high practically all of us are living in the shadow of a totally unpredictable kind of violence.

If anyone had asked me toward the middle of the afternoon what was drawing me, despite all of my better instincts, in the direction of death and violence I'd have come right out and told him.

I had Mars fever too. I hated the Big Lie and all of its ramifications, knew that every charge that was being hurled at the Colonization Board was untrue. But I knew exactly how all of the tormented, desperate men felt, the ones who fought the Big Lie and still had the fever and needed to be cradled in strangeness and vastness—needed space and a new frontier to keep from feeling strapped down, walled in, prisoners in a completely new kind of torture chamber.

The restlessness was growing because Man had lived too long in a closed circuit that had almost destroyed him. The great barrier that was no longer there had brought the world to the brink of a universal holocaust, and just knowing that it had been shattered forever was enabling men and women everywhere to lead healthier lives, set their goals higher.

There was nothing wrong with that. Only—not one man or woman in fifty thousand would see with their own eyes the rust-red plains of Mars, and the play of light and shadow on a world covered over much of its surface with wide zones of abundant vegetation. Not one in fifty thousand would have a new world to rejoice in, after the long journey through interplanetary space. A world laden with springtime scents, in the wake of the crash and thunder of the polar ice caps dissolving.

Or possibly snow piled high on a sleeping landscape, with a thaw just starting, and the prints of small furry creatures on the white blanket of snow, for the first colonists had taken animals with them.

It would take another thirty years for newer, swifter rockets to be built and the supply problem to be brought under control and the colony to outgrow its birth pangs and its tumultuous adolescence and become a white and towering city, as huge as New Chicago.

And there were some who could not wait, for whom waiting was destructive to body and mind, a kind of living death too terrible to be sanely endured.

The fingers of the woman sitting opposite me were becoming restive, tightening a little on my hand. It seemed incredible to me that I could have gone off on that kind of thinking-back tangent when I was so close to paradise.

For paradise was there, seated directly across the table from me, in that crazy twilight hour, if I'd had the courage to seize it boldly—and if I hadn't been still in love with Joan.

I could still make a stab at finding out for sure, I told myself, if I brushed aside the obstacles, if I refused to let my mind dwell on how I'd feel if something happened to Joan and I lost her forever. How could she have been so stubborn and foolish, when she was sophisticated enough to know that no man is insulated against temptation when he is lonely and despairing and paradise can be his for the taking, if he can kill just one part of himself and let the rest survive.

"What is it?" she asked. "You haven't said a word for five minutes. I'm a good listener, you know. I always have been—perhaps too good a listener."

It was the moment of truth, when I had to decide. Mars—and a woman too. Mars—and the big, important job, and the clatter and bright wonder of tremendous machines, with swiftly moving parts, whirring, blurring, dust and the stars of morning, and a woman like that in my arms.

I had to decide.

"What is it?" she asked. "Can't you tell me?"

"Someday I'll tell you," I said. "But not now. I've a feeling we'll meet again. Where and how and when I don't know, because by this time tomorrow I'll be on my way to Mars."

A pained look came into her eyes and she quickly released my hand.

"But we've just started to get acquainted," she protested. "You know nothing about me—or hardly anything. I thought—"

"It might be best not to know," I said, and I think she must have realized then just how it was, must have read the truth in my eyes, for a faint flush suffused her face and she said quickly: "All right. If that's the way it must be."

I nodded and beckoned to the waiter, hoping she wouldn't suspect how vulnerable I still was, how dangerously easy it would have been for me to alter my decision.

Ten minutes later I was alone again, with Lake Michigan glimmering at my back, and only the stars for company. And I still didn't know her name.


## CHAPTER THREE

IT HAPPENED SO SUDDENLY IT WOULD have taken me completely by surprise, if the alarm bell hadn't started ringing again in some shadowy corner of my mind. It wasn't clamorous this time, but it was loud enough to make me straighten in alarm, with every nerve alert.

I was standing by a high wall of foliage, close to the lakeside and had just started to light a cigarette. All at once, directly overhead, there was a rustling sound that was hard to mistake, for I'd heard it many times before, and it had a peculiar quality, which set it apart from all other sounds.

Something was moving through the shadows above me, rustling dry leaves, slithering down toward me with a dull, mechanical buzzing.

The buzzing stopped abruptly and there was a flash of brightness, a long-drawn whining sound. I braced myself, letting my arms swing loosely at my side.

With startling swiftness something long, glistening and snakelike descended upon me and wrapped itself around my right leg just above the knee. Before I could shake it loose it contracted into a tight knot and the whining turned into a shrill scream, prolonged, ghastly. It was quite unlike the scream of an animal. There was something metallic, rasping about it, as if more than animal ferocity was giving voice to its pent-up rage in a shrill mechanical monotone.

The constriction increased and an agonizing stab of pain lanced up my thigh. I raised my right arm and brought the edge of my hand down with an abrupt, chopping motion. I chopped downward three times, not at random, but with a calculated, deadly precision, for I knew that a misdirected blow could have cost me my life.

I was in danger only for an instant, and not a very long instant at that. The damage I'd done to it caused it to release its grip on my leg, shudder convulsively and drop to the ground.

Damaged where it was most vulnerable, it writhed along the ground with groping, disjointed movements of its entire body. Tiny fragments of shattered crystal glistened in its wake, and two long wires dangled from its cone-shaped head.

Its segmented body-case glowed with a blood-red sheen as it writhed across a flat gray stone on the edge of the lakeshore embankment, and reared up for an instant like an enormous, sightlessly groping worm. Then, abruptly, all the animation went out of it, and it flattened out and lay still. Both of the optical disks, which had enabled it to move swiftly through the darkness, had been smashed. I was no longer in any danger and it was very pleasant just to know that.

Very pleasant indeed.

An attempt had been made on my life. There could be no blinking the fact. That little mechanical horror, with its complex interior mechanisms, had been set upon me from a distance with all of its electronic circuits clicking by remote control.

From just how great a distance I had no way of knowing. But I didn't think he'd be staying around, near enough for me to get my hands on him. Killers who made use of such gadgets usually kept their distance, and were very cautious.

But at least I knew now that I had a dangerous enemy, someone who wanted me dead. And there was nothing pleasant about that.

The human mind is a very strange instrument and it's hard to predict just how profoundly you'll be upset by an occurrence that's difficult to dismiss with a shrug.

You can either turn morbid and brood about it, or rise superior to it and pigeonhole it, at least for the moment. By a kind of miracle I was able to pigeonhole it, to keep it from standing in the way of what I'd made up my mind to do before I'd heard the rustling in the foliage directly overhead.

I walked back and forth for a moment, resting most of my weight on my right leg, to make sure I could keep using it without limping and when I was satisfied a long walk wouldn't be in the least painful I left the embankment with a feeling of relief and took the first turn on my left. I was pretty sure it would take me no more than twenty minutes to get back to the spaceport.

I knew that what I'd made up my mind to do wasn't going to be easy. I had to find out exactly how important a job the Colonization Board had mapped out for me on Mars. She'd called me "Mr. Important Man" because—you don't get a clearance stamped the way mine was unless there's a big undertaking in store for you which has to be handled in just the right way. The walk gave me a chance to think about it. My leg didn't trouble me at all and I was very grateful for that...I stood for a moment just outside the spaceport's railed-off, electronically protected launching platforms, staring up at the three-hundred-foot passenger rockets gleaming with a dull metallic luster in the moonlight, their nose-cones pointing skyward.

The New Chicago Spaceport has and always will attract sightseers, because there's no other rocket-launching site on Earth that can compare with it. It's not only the largest and the most elaborately equipped. It was built to last. Fifty years from now, in 2070, say, it was a safe bet the big Mars rockets would be taking off at four-hour intervals night and day. Now they took off only twice a month and there were fifty million people in the United States alone who would have given up comfort, leisure, a well-paying job and every joy they'd ever experienced or could hope to experience on Earth to be on one of those big sky ships.

As far back as I can remember I'd hated to force a showdown with people who trusted me and believed in me. And that went double for the Martian Colonization Board, whose members were doing everything possible to keep me informed. Secrecy sometimes has to be imposed, and if you try to crack an information clampdown prematurely you deserve to be slapped down.

But now I had no choice. I had to find out if my trip could be postponed, if I could wait one more week—a month even —to get Joan to see things my way. And that meant I had to find out just how big a job they had lined up for me.

I had no trouble getting in to see him. There was a guard at the main entrance of the Administration Building, and when I identified myself and the massive, double-doors swung inward I had to go through it a second time, and six more times in all before I reached his private office on the twentieth floor. But you couldn't call it trouble, because all I had to do was take out my wallet and display the pale blue card that was only an incitement to violence in certain quarters.

In that massive, almost half-mile-long building, on every floor, there were guards who knew me and guards who had never set eyes on me before. But what that card stood for was treated with respect.

I'd known that building to hum with activity, to come to life with a roar. But now only one floor blazed with light and the rest of the building was as silent as a mausoleum.

It happens sometimes and when it does everyone is grateful—including the man I'd come to visit.

His private office was at the end of a long corridor in Section C 10 Y, and I knew I'd find him there, because a small circle of cold light had been glowing above the office listing board on the main floor. There was a nameplate above the numbered listings—BROWN. His name wasn't Brown, of course. Or Smith, or Jones. The "Brown" was just a safety precaution—the sign and seal of immense power being modest in a genuine way and for expediency's sake as well.

No man without the kind of card I carried had ever gotten as far as that office listing board and I doubt if the most ingenious assassin would have cared to try. But it was just as well to be on the completely safe side.

A saluting guard stepped back and what was perhaps the narrowest, least impressive door in the entire building opened and closed and I found myself in his presence.

Unless you're a Gobi desert dweller or live in the precise middle of the Sahara you've seen the blue-eyed, mild-mannered little man who was Jonathan Trilling on a hundred lighted screens. In all respects but one, he is the kind of man most people would go right past on the street without a second glance.

The thing that made him really not like that at all was something you couldn't pin down and analyze. If you tried, you'd get nowhere. But it was there, all right, an emanation you couldn't mistake that stamped him for what he was, radiating out from him.

Equate immense simplicity with immense power and you might come up with a part of the answer. But not all of it.

The office was stripped of all non-essentials; a hermit's cell couldn't have been barer. And it seemed to please him when my eyes swept over the almost bare desk, with just an inkwell and a single sheet of paper on it, before coming to rest on his face.

I'm pretty sure he interpreted it as an indication that I was trying to catch him up on something he took pride in, and he admired me for it, and greeted me with a chuckle.

"Well, Ralph!" he said. "I didn't expect to see you here tonight. I thought you'd be home wearing Joan's patience ragged with the kind of last-minute preparations women never seem to understand. They like to think they never forget anything. But they do. They're worse that way than we are, but just try getting them to admit it."

There was only one chair in the office and he was occupying it. I hardly expected him to get up and wave me toward it, but that's precisely what he did.

"Sit down, Ralph," he said. "I sit too much. We all do here, I guess. Can't be helped, but it doesn't give a man of fifty-five much chance to get the exercise he ought to have, if he's going to keep his weight down."

"No—don't get up for me, sir!" I said, then realized I was being unnecessarily formal.

The chair was empty and he expected me to take it. And I could see that he didn't like the "sir." He never had.

"Sit down, sit down. What is it, Ralph'! Something worrying you? You'll have plenty of time for that when you get to Mars. Why start now?"

I decided to come right out with it. I favored bluntness as much as he did, and there was nothing to be gained by talking around what I'd have to ask him before I left.

"There's something I'd like to know," I said. "Is the major part of my assignment still under wraps, or could you tell me more about it—even if you'd prefer not to?"

He looked at me steadily for a moment, his lips tightening a little. "Well—I certainly haven't kept it a complete secret, Ralph. You'll get full instructions in code later on. There's naturally a reason for that. I shouldn't have to go into it, because we've discussed it at great length right here in this office."

"I realize that," I said. "But could you see your way clear to telling me much more than you have, if I can convince you that it would help me solve a problem I can't solve otherwise."

His eyebrows went up a little at that. "What kind of problem, Ralph?"

"It's as old as the hills," I said. "The really ancient kind with fossils embedded in them. It goes right back to, the Old Stone Age, and maybe a lot earlier. Joan doesn't want to go to Mars. She's very stubborn, very determined about it. If I can't make her change her mind I'll have to go alone. And I guess I don't have to tell you what that would do to me. If I just had a little more time, another week or two—"

"So that's it," he said. "You want me to tell you that your assignment can be put off, that you're not really needed on Mars. We're just sending you there because we like to do whimsical things occasionally, to break the God-awful monotony of thinking about the problems the project is confronted with in a serious way."

I was startled, because I'd never known him to indulge in deliberate irony before. He had all the intellectual equipment for it, but his mind just didn't work that way.

Then I suddenly realized he was going to tell me everything I wanted to know and had just used that approach to make me a little angry and keep me alert and analytical, so that I wouldn't underestimate the seriousness of what he was about to say.

"All right, Ralph," he said. "I'll risk angering a third of the Board. I'm going to tell you exactly why the Mars Colony is in trouble, and just how tremendous your task will be. You'll be in the middle, Ralph, in the biggest clash of interests a new and growing society has ever known.

"A clash of interests can destroy any society, if they're violent enough and have powerful enough backing and the population is divided in its loyalties and lacks firm and courageous leadership.

"That's especially true if the society is on a pioneering level, with serious scarcities developing everywhere and with every man, to some extent at least, in fierce competition with his neighbors, all apart from the massive power monopolies that are in even fiercer competition among themselves.

"Don't you see, Ralph, don't you realize what that kind of cross-purpose distribution of power in a new and pioneering society can mean? When you have a three or four-way conflict, when everyone is bidding for what you've got and can't afford to sell, or what you haven't got but would like to sell, or what you can't sell for what you'd like to get?"

He smiled suddenly, for the barest instant, and then the seriously concerned look, which the smile had replaced, came back into his eyes. "I didn't intend that to sound facetious. It probably did, because it has a slightly humorous side to it, like most major tragedies. I'm just giving you the broad outlines now, the general situation. Frustration, bitterness, thousands of colonists who can be swayed one way or the other by corrupt pressures, self-interest, greedy power monopolies."

"But there's a more specific situation you have in mind, is that it?" I asked. "Everything you've just said is common knowledge."

Trilling nodded. "Yes—but the general situation has to be underscored. It is the crucial factor in everything that is taking place on Mars. In a more stable, and highly developed society the raw power conflict of the two major power monopolies would not take so destructive a form."

"Two?" I said. "I was under the impression—"

He waved my objection aside. "Oh, there are a dozen power combines. But only the two giants—Wendel Atomics and Endicott Fuel—have fought each other to a standstill and threaten the peace, and stability of the entire colony. I'm putting it too mildly. There's an explosive potential in that conflict that could destroy the colony overnight."

He tightened his lips and took a turn up and down the office, then came back to where I was sitting and gripped me by the shoulder. "Ralph, listen. This is vital. I'll try to sum it up as briefly as possible. You know what it cost to set up atomic generators, turbines, transmission lines, and keep utilities no city can do without in operation right here in New Chicago, in just one small section of the city? How much more do you think it costs to do the same thing on Mars?

The transportation of materials alone— Have you any idea how much the total expenditures come to?"

"I guess so," I said. "I don't like to think about it."

"Who does? But we had to think about it. We had to give Wendel Atomics a thirty-year monopoly. No other power combine had sufficient monetary resources to undertake it. And we had to give Endicott Fuel the same kind of monopoly. They transport both atomic and liquid fuels at a cost that would turn your hair white."

"And now you say they're locked in a power conflict. But why? I should think Wendel Atomics would purchase all the fuel it needs directly from Endicott. And Endicott would—"

I paused, troubled.

"What would Endicott do, Ralph? It has no use for atomic generators. It isn't geared to install them, even if it could somehow absorb the terrific expense of transporting them. And that, of course, would be impossible. No combine is wealthy enough to undertake that kind of two-pronged enterprise."

"But it wouldn't have to be a two-way exchange of commodities," I said. "Not if Wendel continued to buy all of its fuel from Endicott. It would, of course, have a tendency to dwarf Endicott, make it the lesser of the two monopolies."

"It would do more than that, Ralph. It could bankrupt Endicott. You see, Wendel Atomics suddenly decided it was paying Endicott too much for the fuel it used, and cut the price it was paying in half. And Endicott could barely meet expenses."

"Good Lord," I said.

"Naturally Wendel Atomics couldn't get along without fuel," Trilling said. "And it couldn't transport fuel for its own exclusive use from Earth. The two-pronged enterprise factor again. So Endicott struck back by refusing to sell its fuel to Wendel."

"A complete stalemate, you mean?"

"Not quite, Ralph. If it were, one side or the other would have to give in eventually. Endicott seized on the bright idea of selling atomic and liquid fuel directly to the Colonists. A wildcat kind of madness. The colonists buy the fuel on margin and wait for the price to skyrocket. And every so often it does, because Wendel has to keep its generators operating. It won't buy from Endicott, but it has no choice but to buy from the colonists.

"Do you realize what such wild and dangerous wildcat speculation can do to a new, rough-and-tumble, frontier kind of society, Ralph? The colonists don't know whether they're rich or poor from one day to the next. And with all their desperate needs, their frustrations, their scrambling after scarce goods and services, their fierce competitiveness, they are at each other's throats half of the time."

"I'm beginning to get the picture," I said.

"It's a very ugly picture, Ralph. Wendel Atomics buys its fuel sporadically, cheats, steals, connives, beating the price down artificially and then sending it skyrocketing again. It has its own private police force. Translate—brutal roughnecks who know exactly how to keep the colonists in line and frighten them into selling when the fuel market sags and spending every cent they possess to buy more fuel on speculation when the price soars.

"Endicott doesn't care what happens to the colonists. It's out to make Wendel Atomics come to terms and has methods of its own to keep the colonists inflamed and reckless. The whole situation has even taken on a political cast. There are pro-Wendel colonists, who work hand in glove with the Wendel police and colonists who would willingly lay down their lives in defense of noble, altruistic Endicott. It's the right of everyone to buy fuel on speculation, isn't it?"

"I see," I said. "And my job will be to step right into the middle of all that, and try to bring order out of chaos."

Trilling didn't say anything for a moment. He just looked at me, but his gaze was not unsympathetic.

"There's something I'd like to have you hear, Ralph," he said, when the silence had lengthened between us and become almost minute-long. "We have a new, round-the-clock recording to replace the one we've been transmitting at intervals, night and day, for five years. I won't even ask you how many times you've heard it, because you travel around a lot and must have memorized it word for word. But this one is better, I think. At least, it appeals to me more. A hundred million people will hear it, starting tomorrow. It will be on every tele-screen."

He bent over his desk and removed a miniature tape-recorder from the upper right hand drawer. He set it down on the desk and clicked it on.

"Just one passage I'd like you to listen to, Ralph. Not the whole recording. This is it—"

The voice that came from the tape was a very good reading voice, one of the best I'd ever heard. The man was probably a poet. But the words themselves interested me more.

"...so bright with promise has Man's future become that all of the old animosities, the old hates, will soon seem alien to us and strange. A new world is in the making. Who can deny it? The colonization of Mars has fulfilled the deepest instincts of Man's nature, and provided scope for a growth that is as natural to him as breathing.

"The desire to know more, to explore the unknown, to reach out toward constantly expanding horizons can only be satisfied by boldly accepting what the advance of modern science has brought within our grasp. The colonization of Mars is a tribute to Man's stubborn refusal to be easily discouraged or to let mechanical difficulties, no matter how formidable, stand in his way. A tribute as well to his constructive genius, his daring and breadth of vision."

Trilling clicked the tape recorder off, returned it to his desk, and turned to face me again.

"That, Ralph, is the dream," he said. "You and I know what the reality is like. But the millions who will listen to that recording do not. They still believe—and hope."

I was silent for a moment, not quite sure how he'd take what I was going to say. I went over it in my mind, searching for just the right words. It took me a full minute to find them, but he didn't grow impatient.

"I'm not sure the Board is wise in putting out that kind of propaganda. Or any kind of propaganda. After all, we're not trying to sell Mars to anyone. We're doing something that has to be done—you might almost say we're just trying, in a very earnest way, to plug up a gap in the biggest dam that was ever built, to keep the flood waters from carrying us all to destruction."

"You're wrong, Ralph," he said. "It isn't just propaganda. A dream always has to go striding on ahead of reality. It may seem strange to you, but the reality does not frighten or discourage me. Mars is a new world and on a new world there has to be—not one, but many beginnings."

He paused an instant, then added: "That's why we're sending you to Mars, Ralph. There will have to be another beginning. It won't show too much on the surface. No matter how successful you are, for the colony will remain what it is basically—an experiment in survival. All of a new world's energy will remain, and the turbulence and the hard-to-endure disappointments. But you can help the Colonists go back, and feel the way they did when the first passenger rocket settled down on the red desert sand forty million miles from Earth and the Space Age took on a new dimension."

# CHAPTER FOUR

THERE WAS ONLY ONE SMALL WINDOW in Trilling's office. But I could see that the sky outside was still bright with stars, and the glimmer of the ceiling lamp made the metal surface above us seem to fall away and dissolve into a much wider expanse of star-studded space.

The ceiling-mirrored image of the lamp itself looked like the Sun, blazing in noonday brightness directly overhead and out beyond were galaxies and super-galaxies strung like beads on a wire across the great curve of the universe.

It was just an illusion, of course. You could see the same thing in the light-mirroring depths of a glass of wine, if you stared hard enough. But for an instant it seemed to bring bigness, vastness right into the room with us.

I was conscious of the silence again, lengthening, hanging heavy between us, as if we'd each said too much, or possibly...not quite enough.

Then Trilling bent and removed something else from his desk. I couldn't see what it was until he set it down directly in front of me, because it was much smaller than the midget tape recorder and his hand covered it.

A flat metal box, wafer-thin, doesn't provide much scope for speculation, and I was pretty sure that the object inside was a tiny metal precision instrument or a watch or a medal even before he said: "This should make Joan change her mind, Ralph!" and snapped the box open.

The insignia caught and held the light, a two-inch silver hawk with its wings outspread. The white lining of the box made it stand out, as if it were flying through fleecy clouds high in the sky, and symbolizing in its flight far more than just the elevation of one man to the highest command post the Martian Colonization Board had the authority to bestow.

The significance of that finely wrought, seldom-worn silver bird was not lost on me. In the maze of a hundred legends, a hundred witness-confirmed stories of triumph and disappointment, of heroic progress and tragic backtracking, it had remained an important link between Earthside expectations and what was actually taking place on Mars.

Only one man could wear it at anyone time, and only four men had worn it since the establishment of the colony. All four were dead now, their gravestones a white gleaming on the red desert sand a few miles north of the colony.

"Well, Ralph?" Trilling said.

I tried hard to maintain my composure, to say just the right thing, because I'd lived long enough to know there are depths beyond depths to some emotions that can't be put into words. Attempt to talk the way you feel, and you're sure to sound a little ridiculous. I was only certain of one thing. No man could wear that insignia and not feel, resting upon his shoulders, a responsibility so tremendous that whatever pride he might take in it would have to be tempered by humility—if he wanted to go on wearing it for long.

Trilling seemed aware of what was passing through my mind, for he made it easy for me. He simply smiled, snapped the box shut with a briskness that was almost casual, and handed it to me.

"You've got real massive military prestige now, Ralph," he said. "Right at the moment the Board would be gravely concerned if you wore that insignia in public. But there's nothing to prevent you from wearing it in the privacy of your own home. Later on the Board may decide you can accomplish more by coming right out and letting the colonists know there's a lion in the streets who intends to do more than just roar. A safe, protective kind of lion—dangerous only to over-ambitious men with destructive ideas."

I started to reply but he waved me to silence. "Hold on, Ralph—let me finish. You won't be wearing that insignia in public straight off. But I hope you'll have enough good sense to make the best possible use of it to overcome the first really big obstacle in your path."

He nodded. "It will be a kind of blackmail, in a way—morally reprehensible. You'll be taking advantage of something it isn't in a woman's nature to resist. But you have no choice. You've got to go to Mars and if you went alone you'd be about as useful to us as a celibate kangaroo, all packaged and ready to be sent on a journey to the taxidermist."

He seemed to realize it wouldn't have to be quite that drastic, for he grimaced wryly. "All right, all right. You could go out and find another woman and I probably could talk the Board into being the opposite of stuffy about it. But I happen to know what kind of man you are, and how you feel about Joan. I could be wrong, but I'm pretty sure she's the only woman in the world for you."

There was nothing I could say to that. I had the insignia in my inner breast pocket, and I knew that there were few obstacles it couldn't blast away on Earth or on Mars, if I kept remembering what it symbolized with Joan at my side.

I went out into the cool night again, past that long tremendous building with just one of its floors ablaze, past the big sky ships looming like sentinel ghosts on their launching pads, past winking lights and speeding cars and pedestrians walking slowly and something inside of me made me feel I'd undergone a kind of sea change, and could face whatever the future might hold without grabbing for a lifeline that didn't exist.

It was a good way to feel. A man had to sink or swim without having a lifeline thrown to him—if he hoped to live long enough to change things around in an important way on

Mars. He had to keep his head and breast the raging currents with the sturdiest kind of overhand strokes, or be drawn down into the undertow and battered senseless against the rocks that lined the shoreline.

The change must have shown a little on the surface, in the set of my jaw or just the way I was walking, because no less than three pedestrians turned to stare at me as I went striding past them on my way to the New Chicago Underground.

I was almost at the northern entrance of the big, tree-lined square directly opposite the Administration Building when it hit me—the memory-recall, the swift emergence from its cubby-hole deep in my mind of the narrow brush I'd had with Death and hadn't even discussed with Trilling.

It had been a mistake not to discuss it, because it concerned the Board as much as it did me. Someone who knew about the insignia—or had made a shrewd guess as to just how big a job was awaiting me on Mars—had wanted me dead. The attempt on my life took on a much larger, more crucial dimension when viewed in that light.

There were three hundred million people in the United States, and if I'd been just a private citizen, with no more than my own safety at stake, I could have lost myself in that immense ocean of humanity for a week or a month and gained a brief respite. There are plenty of ways you can protect yourself against a surprise attempt on your life, if you have the time to take safety precautions. When there's a would-be assassin at large who is dead set on measuring you for a coffin you have to work the problem out carefully, with a minimum of risk.

It takes skill and psychological insight, but it can be done. You've just got to remember that an assassin is never quite normal. Even when a socio-political motivation is the governing passion of his life you're one jump ahead of him the instant you've figured out exactly how his mind works.

In fact, one of those safety precautions could have been protecting me as I crossed the square, if I hadn't let my stubborn pride stand in the way. Why hadn't I asked Trilling to provide me with armed protection?

Two alert bodyguards, trailing me on the street and down into the Underground and standing watch outside my apartment all night long—and staying fifty paces behind me until the Mars' rocket zero-count ended and the big sky ship took off with a roar…would have given the Board the kind of reassurance they had a right to expect.

I started to turn back, then changed my mind abruptly. I'd taken just as great a risk by walking from the lakeside to the skyport right after the attack, hadn't I? And I'd be in the Underground in another three or four minutes, with people around me and—

All right. It was an out-of-focus rationalization and nothing more—an attempt to find an excuse for not turning back. But when I do something reckless for complicated reasons, when I've forged ahead despite my better judgment, I'm usually just impulsive enough to carry the folly-ball all the way across the goal line.

It was the thing I'd have to guard most against on Mars, that damnable twisted pride and impulsiveness, that taking of too much for granted when I started to do something I knew was unwise, but had an overpowering urge to carry out anyway.

Every weaving shadow beneath the double row of trees that towered on both sides of me could have cloaked a crouching figure adjusting another small mechanical killer to the deadliest possible angle of flight. But I had another reason for not wanting to go back. Trilling might fall in with the armed guard idea but I doubted it like hell. I could picture him saying instead: "Ralph, even an armed car can be blown up. You're staying under lock and key all night...right here in the Administration Building."

I could even picture him saying much the same thing to Joan, her image bright enough on his office tele-screen to be visible from where I'd be standing: "He's not coming home tonight, Joan. We're sending an armored car to pick you up in the morning. Wait, hold on—I'll let you talk to him!"

And I could almost hear her replying: "Don't bother to send the car. I'm not going with him. Please don't think too harshly of me, please try to understand. I just can't—"

I started down the long boulevard on the far side of the square, still walking rapidly and feeling suddenly confident I'd been justified in not turning back. I could see the entrance to the Underground glimmering in the darkness a hundred feet ahead of me and there were people all around me walking in both directions. I wasn't even troubled by the feeling that everyone gets at times—that something terrible and unexpected can happen right in the midst of a crowd, if only because the presence of many people exposes you to a dangerously wide range of unpredictable human emotions.

For the barest instant, when I crossed the narrow strip of pavement directly in front of the kiosk, fear tugged at my nerves and I felt myself growing tense. But I became calm again the moment I looked around and saw that the only pedestrian within thirty feet of me was a hurrying girl with a portfolio under her arm. When she saw how intently I was staring at her she frowned and a look of annoyance came into her eyes.

Oh, for God's sake, I told myself, get rid of this nagging uncertainty, and stop behaving like a fool. If he intended to try again tonight I'd know by now. He's missed a dozen very good chances, so something must be making him super-cautious, if he hasn't keeled over just from the strain of watching me refuse to die. Killing's never easy, even for a professional. It must be a little like being cut open, watching your own blood pouring out of you, because all violence inflicts a two-way trauma…severe enough at times to make even a mad slayer fling down his gun before going on a rampage of indiscriminate slaughter.

There were arguments I could have used to wrap it up even tighter—such as the way he'd be trapped and blasted down almost instantly if he launched another attack on me so close to the spaceport's three interlocking, hyper-sensitive security alert systems.

But I didn't even pause to weigh them, because right up to that minute I'd done very well, and the fear which had come upon me had been as brief as an autumnal flurry of wind when you're coming around a tall building at breakneck speed.

I let the girl dart past me, taking my time, and in another five seconds was descending into the big, brightly-lighted cavern that was New Chicago's intercity pride.

As every school kid knows, the New Chicago Underground is six years old, and is the largest, smoothest-running transportation system in the world. It cost seven billion dollars to build and has almost as many tracks and suburban offshoots as station guards.

It interlocks, spirals outward in a half dozen directions and circles back upon itself. In a way, it's like the serpent you see in bas-reliefs dating back three thousand years, in Babylonian and Pre-Dynastic Egyptian tombs, for instance, or on totem poles in the Northwest…a serpent that's continually swallowing its own tail. It's the oldest archeological art form on Earth and is supposed to symbolize Eternal Life.

But to some people at least the New Chicago Underground symbolizes something far more gloomy. If you're not careful to board just the right train you can get lost in its tomblike, spiraling immensity and feel as helpless as a wandering ghost or an experimental laboratory animal caught up in a blind maze. You can be carried fifty miles in the wrong direction and look out through the windows of a train traveling at half the speed of sound, and see a country landscape or the wide sweep of Lake Michigan five minutes after you've settled down in a comfortable chair and become absorbed in the news of the day on micro-film.

You'll stare out and the section of the city where your home is located just won't be sweeping past. You'll have to get off at the next station, perhaps twenty or thirty miles further on, ride back, and board another train. It's seldom quite as frustrating as that, but only because most of the riders have been conditioned to keep their wits about them through a nightmare kind of trial-and-error apprenticeship.

You've got to stay alert until you've boarded a train with just the right combination of numerals on its destination plate. It isn't hard to do, unless you're carrying a tiny silver hawk in a wafer-thin case, and your destination may be changed without warning and with unbelievable infamy by someone capable of great evil who would much prefer not to have you board a train at all.

I could almost picture him weaving in and out between the platform crowds—faceless so far, but quite possibly glassy-eyed with little waltzing death-heads in the depth of his pupils. An unknown human cipher intent on my destruction, refusing to be discouraged by the failure of a small mechanical killer to do the job for him.

If I'd had a strong reason to believe I actually was being followed, if he'd come right out into the open and I could have caught a glimpse of him, however brief, I'd have felt a subconscious relief, that would have kept me on guard and confident. It would have given me an edge that not even the fact that I had no gun could have taken away from me.

It's the unknown and unpredictable that's unnerving, the realization that invisible eyes may be scrutinizing you from a distance and the brain behind them deciding that it would be a great mistake to let a failure of nerve or concern for the consequences interfere with what had to be done.

He wouldn't be wanting me to wear that insignia ever—on Earth or on Mars—and just knowing that made me almost miss my train as it came rushing toward me.

The train was so crowded I had to stand, but I had no complaint on that score. In a seat, with people jamming the aisle in front of me, I'd have been wedged in even more securely. In a standing position I could edge forward and back and keep an eye on the passengers who were holding fast to the horizontal support rail on both sides of me.

## CHAPTER FIVE

THERE WERE TWENTY-FIVE OR THIRTY passengers wedged into the middle section of the train, all standing in slightly cramped postures and most of them unsmiling. I knew exactly how they felt. Not being able to get a seat in an off-hour in the evening can be irritating. But right at the moment there was no room in my mind for annoyance. A slow, hard-to-pin-down uneasiness was creeping over me again, as if a pendulum were swinging back and forth somewhere close to me, ticking out a warning in rhythm—- and I couldn't shut out the sound of it.

Just my over-strained nerves, of course. How could it have been anything else? I turned and looked at the man standing next to me. He was middle-aged, conservatively dressed, and had a square-jawed, rather handsome face, with a dusting of gray at his temples.

He was frowning slightly and his expression didn't change when I broke the rule of silence that was customarily observed in the Underground.

"No reason for all the seats to be gone at this hour," I said.

The crazy kind of over-exuberance mixed with peevishness that makes some people say things like that to total strangers a dozen times a day had always seemed inexcusable to me. But when you're under tension you sometimes break all the habits of rational behavior you've imposed on yourself in small matters.

My excuse was that I simply wanted to test the firmness and steadiness of my own voice, to make sure that, deep down, I wasn't nearly as apprehensive as I was beginning to feel.

"Yes, I know," the gray-templed man agreed. "It burns me up a little too. But I guess it just can't be helped at times. Operating an Underground this size must be an awful train-scheduling headache."

"Headache or not," I said. "There's no excuse for it."

He smiled abruptly, exposing large, white teeth and I noticed that there was something almost birdlike in the way his eyes lighted up. Small, black, very bright eyes they were, under short-lashed lids, and quite suddenly he made me think of a magpie alighting on a limb, taking off and alighting again, hardly able to restrain an impulse to chatter.

"What it boils down to," he said, "is the old quarrel between a pedestrian and a man in a car. Neither can understand nor sympathize with the other's point of view. Fifteen million people ride this Underground every day and to them it's a poor slob's service at best. That's because they feel themselves to be the victims, at the receiving end. But you've got to remember that safety precautions pose a problem. Avoiding accidents comes first and the New

Chicago Transportation System, considering its colossal size, does pretty well in that respect."

"People have been killed," I said, and could have bitten my tongue out. Why let him even suspect that I was thinking about something that wasn't tied in with his argument at all, why give him the slightest hint? The Underground's accident record was good and couldn't have justified such cynicism on my part. And just suppose he wasn't the garrulous, middle-aged businessman he appeared to be—

A very sinister game can start in just that way, with everything favoring the alerted party until he lets the other know that he's on his guard and is having uneasy thoughts. That's where the danger lies, in a subconscious betrayal, a slip of the tongue that will precipitate violence faster than it would ordinarily occur.

If a killer feels that he must move swiftly, before suspicion can become a certainty, the odds shift in his favor. He has the advantage of surprise. He becomes alerted too, and necessity acts as a goad—a kind of trigger-mechanism. He'll act more quickly and decisively, without the careful planning that may prompt him to talk too much and give himself away.

He'll take risks that are dangerous and could destroy him, strike with witnesses present and all escape routes blocked. If he has to, he'll strike even in a crowded Underground train with the next station minutes away. And that kind of audacity sometimes pays off.

I told myself that I was imagining things, jumping to a completely unwarranted conclusion. The conversation of the man next to me was exactly what you'd expect from a magpie. He was carefully sidestepping all realistic appraisals of the Underground's shortcomings, trying his best to look at the problem from all sides, even if it meant being shallow and over-optimistic. He was the citizen with a smiling face, the rather likeable guy—why should one hold it against him?—

who was trying his best to be fair to everybody, even if he had to burst a blood-vessel doing it.

Realizing all that made me feel less tense and part of the nightmare feeling I'd been experiencing went away. But not quite all of it and when the train passed into an unlighted tunnel and the aisle went dark apprehension began to mount in me again.

What if he was putting on an act, and wasn't the kind of man he appeared to be at all? What does a killer look like? Certainly age had nothing to do with it. He can be young or old-eighteen or seventy-five.

His appearance, his clothes? There were wild-eyed killers with "psycho" stamped all over them, and dignified, soberly dressed men who looked no different from your next door neighbor and had criminal records a yard long, including, in all likelihood, a murder or two the Law would have a difficult time proving.

I didn't have to speculate about it. I *knew,* because I'd done more than my share of social research. There was nothing to prevent a man of distinction from becoming a killer, if he had a secret life that was ugly and devious and a powerful enough motive.

But now he was talking again, despite the darkness, and I was listening with my nerves on edge. I was completely in the dark as to why something about him had set the alarm bells ringing but I was sure I could hear them, very faint and distant this time, but clearly enough. It was funny. Sometimes it meant something and sometimes it didn't. I could feel that danger was hovering right at my elbow and in the end discover I'd been completely mistaken.

I hoped I was mistaken this time, but I knew there was a possibility—remote, perhaps, but dangerous to ignore—that the man who had set the small mechanical killer in motion by the Lakeside had followed me from the Administration Building into the Underground and was standing by my side.

"You take one of the really big power combines," he was saying. "Like, say, Wendel Atomics. It has its defenders and detractors, and I daresay there are quite a few people who would be happy to see its Board of Directors behind bars. I'm not defending the Wendel monopoly, understand. If I was a Martian colonist I might feel quite differently about it. But you've got to remember that when you give the go-ahead signal for a project that big you're asking fifty or a hundred key executives to do the impossible—or pretty close to the impossible."

"The impossible?" I said, trying to sound no more than mildly interested, because I didn't want him to suspect what a jolt his mention of Wendel Atomics had given me.

"Oh, yes," he went on. "That's what it boils down to. Every one of those men will be as human as you or I. They'll react in highly individual ways to every problem that comes up, every frustration, every serious interference with their private lives. You've got to remember that a man's private life is the most important thing in the world—to him personally. Everyone of those fifty or a hundred men will have health worries, money worries, love life worries, every kind of worry you can think of. And on Mars worries can pile up."

"So I've heard," I said.

"Well, that's all. That sums it up. I'm simply citing Wendel as an example of what the New Chicago Transportation System is up against. I'd say, in general, that most of the directors are doing their best, when the Old Adam in them isn't in the driver's seat, to keep the trains running on schedule."

He stopped talking abruptly. I didn't think anything of it for a moment, for a loquacious man will often pause in the middle of a conversation to wonder what kind of dent he's been making on the party who's doing most of the listening. But when a full minute passed and the darkness held, and he didn't say a word, when I couldn't even hear him breathing, I began to grow uneasy.

Reach out and touch him? Well, why not? It was the simplest, quickest way of finding out whether he was still at my side and he could hardly be offended if my hand grazed his elbow in a jostling motion that would seem accidental.

It was very strange. I didn't think he was the man I'd feared he might be any longer, because of what he'd said, because he *had* brought Wendel Atomics into the conversation. If he'd had designs on my life giving his hand away like that would have been the height of folly. It would have been like giving me cards and spades, and a detailed history of his activities for the past five years.

It didn't take any gifted reasoning to figure that out and I didn't pride myself on it. Even a child could have done it. What disturbed me and kept me from feeling relieved was something quite different. The alarm bells were still ringing. *They were still ringing.*

Louder now and with a dirgelike persistence, as if I was already dead and buried. And neither a child nor a grown man could have figured that one out.

That's why I felt I had to reach out and touch him, had to start him talking again…had to be sure he was still there at my side.

He was there, all right. He was there in the most alarming possible way, as a dead weight lurching against me, then swaying and screaming as I tried to straighten him up, and stop the terrible downward drag of his sagging body.

He was sinking lower and lower, clutching at my knees now, refusing to take advantage of the support I was offering him. I strained and tugged, but it was no use. He was too heavy to raise and I could hear the breath wheezing out of his throat and there could be no mistaking the weight of horror that was making him twist and writhe as he sagged—the deadliness of whatever it was that had struck at him in the darkness without making a sound.

He screamed again. It was the kind of agonized protest which could only have come from the throat of a man who hardly knew what was happening to him...a man with his terror heightened and made more acute by the awful, groping-in-the-dark realization that he was experiencing a torment he was powerless to explain.

There had to be an answer but I didn't know what it was, and when the scream died away and the tugging stopped all I could hear for an instant was the steady droning of the train. Then there was another violent movement close to me and a harsh intake of breath.

My hand shot out, grazed something smooth that whipped away from me and caught hold of a wrist that was much thinner than a man's wrist had any right to be.

Much softer too, velvety soft, and it tugged and jerked in a frantic effort to free itself, holding tight to the knife that it would have taken all of a woman's strength to plunge deep into my heart.

But she could have done it, whoever she was, for there was a wiry strength in her—a strength so great that I had to twist her wrist cruelly before her fingers relaxed and the knife dropped to the floor of the train.

She gasped in pain—or was it fury?—and exerted all of her strength again in a desperate effort to break my grip. And this time luck was on her side. No, call it what it was. Luck may have figured, but most of it was plain blundering stupidity on my part. I was pretty sure I knew what her first, misdirected blow with the knife had done to the man I'd been talking to, and the thought so sickened and unnerved me that my fingers relaxed a little when the knife went clattering, and she took advantage of that to break free.

The passengers were crowding me now, pushing, shoving in alarm, and I knew it would be easy enough for her to force her way between them, still exerting all of her strength and get far enough away to be just one of the thirty terrified people when the train roared out into the light again. They'd all look disheveled, on the verge of panic and I wouldn't have a chance of identifying her.

How could I have identified her with any certainty, even if she'd been the only one with a guilty stare? I hadn't the least idea what she looked like. I only knew that she wasn't old, was all woman in her lithe softness, the opposite of an Amazon despite her strength. The femininity which had emanated from her—how instantly it can make itself felt, how instinctively overwhelming it can be!—had made me feel like a brute for an instant, even though I'd known it was her life or mine and I would have been quite mad to spare her.

There were men I could think of, the opposite of brutes, who would have knocked her unconscious with a blow to the head. To spare a determined killer is potentially suicidal, but I doubted if I could have done that.

I was still doubting it an instant later, when the train emerged from the unlighted tunnel and the bright glare of the Underground lamps flooded the aisle, bringing the man she'd stabbed by accident into clear view.

I was sure by now that she'd stabbed him by accident in a try for me, but that wasn't going to help him at all. He had flopped over on his back and was lying sprawled out in the middle of the aisle, and his eyes stared up at me, sightless and glazed.

There was no blood either on or beside him, but that only meant that he'd been stabbed in the back and there hadn't been time for blood from the wound to stain the edge of his clothes and trickle out from beneath him across the aisle.

His face had the pallor of death and his lips were drawn back over the large white teeth I'd noticed when he'd been talking to me. Drawn back in a stiff, unnatural grin and I didn't have to bend down and listen for a heartbeat I knew I wouldn't hear to be completely sure that the words he'd spoken to me would be the last he'd ever speak on Earth.

Just the way his head lolled, back and forth with the rhythmic throbbings of the train, would have clinched it for me. And I couldn't have bent down, because the other passengers were all staring at him too now, and elbowing me away from him to get a closer look, torn between morbid curiosity and stark terror.

I was too shaken, too sick at heart, to resent the elbowing. There was anger in me too; cold, uncompromising and right at that moment I could no longer even think of her as a woman.

It was past midnight when I got home and let myself into the apartment. I was more shaken than I would have cared to admit to anyone who didn't know me as well as Trilling did, because casual acquaintances can do you an injustice and judge the extent of your control by the way you happen to be looking at the moment.

I was quite sure that I was looking *very* bad, and however severely I'd been shaken up by what had happened I still had a fair measure of control over my emotions.

I hadn't stayed in the train or on the platform to assist in the investigation, but I didn't feel guilty about it. Trilling could square all that with the authorities easily enough and he wouldn't have wanted me to talk to the police and have to identify myself. I was sure of that. My evidence would be taken down and turned over to the proper authorities in good time. The rule for me—the only rule I had a right to consider—was no entanglements.

I shut and locked the front door and almost called out: "It's me, darling!" as I usually do when I come home late, because when Joan is alone in the apartment and hears a door opening and closing she gets angry when I just walk in unannounced. It's part woman-curiosity, part fear, I guess—the thought that it could be a prowler and why should she be kept in suspense while I'm hanging up my hat and coat?

But this time something prevented me from calling out. Possibly the quarrel we'd had was still rankling a little deep in my mind and I wasn't quite sure how she'd take the "Darling."

My stubborn pride again. Or possibly it was just the feeling I had that the apartment was quieter than usual, that when you're keyed up and alert enough to hear a pin drop and you hear nothing—just a stillness that's a little on the weird side—your anxiety becomes too great to be relieved by calling out a cheery greeting.

I felt somehow that it would be wiser, and set better with the way I felt, if I just hung up my coat and walked into the living room without saying a word.

So I walked into the living room without saying a word and she was sitting right in the middle of it, on a straight-back chair with all of her bags packed and standing on the floor by the window, and with all of my bags packed and standing cheek-by-jowl with hers, and the three trunks that were going with me to Mars all sealed up and double-locked, and she wasn't angry or shaking her head or looking at the luggage with scorn.

There was pride in her lustrous brown eyes and the adorable tilt of her chin, and a warmth and a tenderness, and she was smiling at me and nodding.

"Oh, darling," she said. "Darling...darling...come here. Did you think I'd ever let you go to Mars without me? It was just talk—just stubborn, wild, crazy talk and it didn't mean a thing."

If you marry a woman like Joan and ever have a moment of doubt...well, it means you ought to have your head examined. But you're twice as far removed from sanity if you throwaway the check. For you can always be sure it will be redeemed eventually, in full measure and brimming over.

I didn't even have to put on my uniform and attach the small silver hawk to it.

## CHAPTER SIX

WE WERE NOT THE ONLY PASSENGERS in the eight-cabined forward section of the big sky ship, which had been assigned to us. But it had taken us almost a week to get acquainted. To get really acquainted, that is, so that we could relax and feel at ease and really enjoy one another's company.

We were sitting in lounge chairs on the long promenade deck that ran parallel with all eight of the cabins, staring out through translucent crystal at a wide waste of stars.

Sitting in the first chair was a tall, sturdily built man of thirty-eight, with keen blue eyes and a dusting of gray at his temples. His name was Clifton Maddox and he was an electronic engineer. He had stories on tap that could turn your hair white, because he had been to Mars and back eight times.

Seated next to him, with her hand resting lightly on his arm, was a woman in her early twenties, with honey-blonde hair and eyes that held unfathomable glints and an enigmatical ingenuousness that could keep a man guessing in an exciting way. Her name was Helen Melton and she had eyes only for the man at her side. She had managed to make of the trip a continuous honeymoon, despite a few lovers' quarrels and the stern exactions, which her work as a medical laboratory technician had imposed, on her.

I mention these two because they were fairly typical of the group as a whole. They were all unusual individuals, the kind of people you take a liking to straight off, when you meet them casually at a party and exchange a few words with them that you keep remembering for days.

Joan and I sat in the last two chairs on the promenade deck, a little apart from the others. Joan was deep in a book and a little weary of talking and I...was thinking about the robots.

The robots were a story in themselves—a story that could bear a great deal of re-telling. If right at that moment I'd had a son—a bright and eager lad of six or eight—I'd have set him on my knee and talked about the robots.

The five hundred passengers in the big sky ship were not alone in the long journey through interplanetary space. In the last years of the twentieth century, I'd have taken pains to make very clear to him, and in the early years of the twenty-first, a great new science had grown from an infant into a giant.

The science of cybernetics, of giant computers that could do much of Man's thinking for him on a specialized technological level, had transformed the face of the Earth and was continuing to transform it at a steadily accelerating pace.

The rocket's four giant computers were of the newest and most efficient type—humanoid in aspect, with conical heads, massive metal body-boxes, and three-jointed metal limbs which had all of Man's flexible adaptability in the carrying out of complex and difficult tasks.

Robot-like and immense, they towered in the chart room with their six-digited metal hands on their metal knees, their electronic circuits clicking, their tiers of memory banks in constant motion, but otherwise outwardly indifferent to the human activity that was taking place around them.

Four metal giants in a metal rocket, functioning cooperatively with Man in the gulfs between the planets, might have made an imaginative fiction writer of an earlier age catch his breath and glory in the fulfillment of a prophecy. An H. G. Wells perhaps, or an Olaf Stapledon. But the reality was an even greater tribute to the human mind's inventive brilliance than the Utopian dream had been.

The four giant computers were capable of solving problems too technical for the human mind to master without assistance, usually with astounding swiftness and always with the more-than-human accuracy of thinking machines whose prime function was to correlate without error the data supplied to them on punched metallic tapes, and to perform intricate mechanical tasks based upon that data.

The robots were tremendous, by any yardstick you might care to apply, and if I'd had a son—

I stopped thinking about the robots abruptly and sat very still, listening. A sound I'd heard a moment before had come again, much louder this time—a chill, unearthly screeching.

The chart room was just outside the eight-cabin section and I could hear the sound clearly. My nerves again, my over-stimulated imagination?

In space strange and unusual sounds are as common as pips on a radar screen. It was queer how quickly you got used to them. You had to walk around with your ears plugged up, in a sense, but the plugs didn't have to be inserted. They were just natural growths inside your ears— invisible and without substance, but plugs notwithstanding. They produced a kind of psychosomatic deafness, which didn't otherwise interfere with your hearing.

Just the very unusual sounds, the totally inexplicable raspings, dronings, creakings—usually of short duration—were blotted out.

You didn't hear them unless something deep in your mind whispered: "This one is different. This is an emergency. Take heed!"

The screeching was very different. It was like nothing I'd ever heard before, on Earth or in space.

The others must have heard it too, for it had been too loud, the second time, to be ignored. But apparently that strange acceptance of strange noises in space, which goes with the kind of deafness I've mentioned, had only been shattered for me. The six men and women in the lounge chairs had looked a little startled for a moment and exchanged puzzled glances. Which meant, of course, that they had heard it despite the mental earplugs in some inner recess of their minds. But that didn't prevent them from shrugging it off and resuming their conversation.

Joan also looked a trifle uneasy. She stopped reading just long enough to raise her eyes and frown, then became absorbed in the book again.

I got up quietly and pressed her wrist. "See you," I said. She shut the book abruptly and straightened in her chair. "Where are you going, Ralph?"

"Just stay right where you are, kitten," I said. "I'll be back in a moment."

"That screeching noise," she said. "I was wondering about it, Ralph. I guess you'd better see what's causing it."

So she'd been disturbed by it too, and ignoring it had taken a deliberate effort of will which I hadn't realized she was exerting. It made me happy in an odd inner way, because it proved again what I'd always known...that we were very close and there were currents of understanding which flowed back and forth between us and I had a wife I could be proud of.

"It's probably nothing," I said, not wanting to alarm her. "But I might as well take a look. It seems to becoming from the chart room."

"All right," she said and squeezed my hand.

I had to open and shut two sliding panels and pass along a blank-walled passageway to get to the chart room. To my surprise the door was standing open. It's usually kept locked, because there's no section of the sky ship where a man who didn't want anyone to suspect that he harbored within himself the most dangerous kind of destructive impulses could do more damage.

The shattering of a photo-electric eye or the ripping out of a single live connection in just one of the four cybernetic robots could have wrecked the rocket, and sent it spiraling down through the space gulfs in flaming ruin, depending on just how vital to the robot's functioning the shattered part happened to be.

There was a security alert system which would have to be disconnected first, but anyone resourceful enough to get inside the chart room at all, without identification-disk proof that he had a right to be there, would have known precisely how to take care of the preliminary obstacles.

I didn't waste any time in getting to that wide-open door, for my mind was racing on ahead of me like the most alerted kind of alarm system, its jangling warning me that every second counted and that what I dreaded most might very well be true.

What I actually saw, when I reached the doorway and stood there looking in, took me completely by surprise. It wasn't the way I'd pictured it at all. But it was just as unnerving, just as much of a threat to the safety of the ship and it startled me so I must have looked almost comic, standing there idiot-still. But there was nothing comic about what I saw.

The woman I'd almost asked to go to Mars with me was staring straight at me, her hair still piled up high, a look of terrified appeal in her eyes. She wasn't alone. She was struggling furiously with a crewman I'd talked to a few times and neither liked nor disliked—a heavyset man with high cheekbones and pale blue eyes. He was gripping her savagely by the wrist and they were both backed up against one of the robot giants.

Suddenly as I stared her head went back and a convulsive trembling seized her. She began to scream.

## CHAPTER SEVEN

IT WAS A CHRIST-AWFUL MOMENT for her and for me. For her because she had no right to be in the Chart Room, or even on the ship, as far as I knew, and there was a look on the crewman's face that chilled me to the core of my being. It went beyond the anger of a duty-obsessed man, outraged by her infringement of the regulations. It was a completely different kind of anger. There was a savage cruelty, a killing rage in his eyes, impossible to misinterpret.

It was just as awful a moment for me, because I wasn't sure I could get to him before he broke her wrist or did something worse to her. I'd seen a woman kneed in the groin once, by just such an enraged human animal, and the memory of it had never left me. A strong man, turned maniacal, could kill with his hands in a matter of seconds. I'd seen that happen too, and the victim hadn't been a woman, but a man as powerful as the killer.

I crossed the Chart Room in a running leap, grabbed him by the shoulders and swung him about, raining blows on him more or less at random. I just tried to hit him as hard as I could without caring much where the blows landed, so long as they resounded with a meaty smack where they would do the most good. My only aim was to stun and, if possible, cripple him in a terrible, punishing way, so that he'd release his grip on the wrist of the woman he'd been trying to hurt before she screamed again and her hand dangled with a sickening limpness, making me want to permanently demolish him in slow and painful stages.

For a moment I was only sure of one thing. My fist had smashed very solidly into his face at least twice and drawn blood. I could see the gleam of blood on his jaw as he reeled back, and I was almost sure I'd heard his nose crack. There was nothing wrong with that, but it didn't satisfy me. I wanted to turn his face into quivering jelly. But most of all I was hoping, praying that she'd break free before I set about doing that, because a voice was screaming deep in my mind that if she couldn't he might still be capable of injuring her cruelly.

She broke free. Just how I don't know, because the punishment I'd dished out hadn't stunned him. He could still have fractured her wrist, judging by the look of blazing fury he trained on me.

His determination to repay me in full probably explained it. He needed both of his hands free for that, because I could see that what he would have liked to do most was get a strangler's grip on my throat.

The human windpipe doesn't fracture easily, as every experienced medical examiner knows. It's elastic and it gives, and post-mortem appearances prove that you can die by strangulation with your windpipe intact. But I have a horror of anything like that, and I didn't intend to let his fingers come anywhere near my throat.

I smashed my fist into his groin twice, putting so much shoulder-to-elbow resilience into the blows that he bent almost double, wrapped his arms about his middle just above his groin and went staggering backwards.

They were below-the-belt beltings, but I didn't give a damn about that. Manhandling a woman just because she hasn't the strength of a male has always seemed to be just about the worst crime on the books. All right...attacking a child is worse but you certainly forfeit all right to Queensberry Rules consideration when you're called to account for using your strength against anyone weaker than yourself, unless he or she has done something vicious and there's a hell of a good justification for it.

I no longer wanted to permanently demolish him, now that she'd broken free. But I had no control over what happened. The deck of the Chart Room is all smooth metal, and the polishing preparation that's used to keep it bright makes it almost as skid-slippery as a skating rink, if you happen to be thrown a little off-balance.

He was off-balance just enough to change his backward lurch from a stagger to a swaying, spinning glide that sent him crashing against the base of a robot giant.

Up to that instant the four robot giants had looked exactly alike. But a robot in motion looks quite different from a robot at rest, with its massive metal hands on its metal knees, and its gleaming central section in an upright position. The crash was followed by a splintering sound, which continued for several seconds without stopping. There was a whirring as well, and a blinding flash of light came from the metal giant's conical head. Almost instantly the robot was in motion, and the way it swayed as it raised its segmented right arm high into the air so alarmed me that I shouted a warning to the man I'd just finished trying to send to the sick bay for a stay of at least two weeks.

The jerky, erratic way the robot giant was swaying could only mean that the crash had damaged its internal gadgetry, and it had gone completely out of control. It was shaking and quivering all over and even its ponderous central section seemed to bulge a little, as if from hunger-bloat.

That, of course, was absurd. But it's natural enough to think of a robot as human and take refuge in absurdity when you know that a cybernetic brain, encased in a functional body, can do just as much damage as a madman running amuck with a deadly weapon. Just as much...more...when it's out of control.

You don't want to face up to it squarely, you shrink from it, because some instinct tells you it would be dangerous to let the horror of it come sweeping into your mind too fast. So you take refuge in absurdity, you imagine things that are a little on the ludicrous side. A hunger-bloat, a maniacal glare in photoelectric eyes.

But when you've done that, you have to stand and watch the horror take place before your eyes and in the end you've gained nothing...because when anything as terrible as what I saw sears its way into your brain the memory of it will remain with you until you die.

The robot giant's massive metal hand swept downward, descending on the head and shoulders of the man who'd crashed into it. It hurled him to the deck, and flattened him out with a hammer blow that crushed his skull, broke his ribs, and tore a deep gash in his back. A red stain spread over his ripped shirt. I shut my eyes, sickened. There was a screaming behind me. I swung dully about and went to her and held her head against my chest, stroking her hair, whispering soothing words into her ear. I could do that without endangering the safety of the sky ship, because the robot giant had ceased to move. With the descent of its hand all of the whirrings had ceased and it remained in a bent-over position, utterly rigid, its mace-like metal palm still resting on the unstirring crewman's back.

I was quite sure that no jury on Earth would have held me criminally responsible for his death. It had been brought about by an accident I couldn't have foreseen. Every man has the right to defend himself when he's under attack, and not just my own life had been in danger. There was no doubt in my mind...not the slightest... His rage had been homicidal and he would have killed me if I'd given him the chance.

Justifiable homicide. There could be no other verdict, if the insignia the Board had given me hadn't conferred legal immunity when an accidental death stemmed from my right to stay alive and I had been forced to return to Earth and clear myself in court.

I felt no moral guilt, but still—I was badly shaken. I had been instrumental in causing his death, however unintentionally, and it's always better if a man can live out his life without experiencing the deep sadness that goes with that kind of knowledge.

The only difference is—moral guilt never leaves you and grows worse with the years. But there are so many tragic sadness' in life that they have a way of merging into one big, onrushing stream and when you measure that stream against a brighter one, the joy-stream, the scales seem to stay just about even, with the balance maybe just a little heavier on the joyful side.

Right at the moment there was another big, onrushing stream running parallel with the sadness. The sober-obligation stream. Or maybe duty-stream would be a better name for it. We spend at least a third of our lives immersed in it up to our necks and swimming against the toughest kind of currents. Sometimes I think we could do without it entirely.

What was it Baudelaire said about boredom? "But well you know that dainty monster, thou, hypocrite reader, fellow man, my brother." You could practically say the same thing about duty.

But the stream is there, and if you just stay on the bank watching the other swimmers you won't really have the right to plunge into the joy-stream with a clear conscience.

The first thing I had to do was get her out of the Chart Room before she collapsed. She was close to hysteria and I didn't even want her to look at the body again. I was careful to stand between her and the robot, and when I guided her gently toward the door I kept my hand on the back of her head and kept her face pressed to my chest.

It was more difficult than it would have looked on a cinema screen—more awkward and less romantic, and that was the way I wanted it to be, because nothing could have been further from my mind at that moment than the romantic glow I'd felt when I had been sitting across a table from her in a lakeside tavern on Earth, and hadn't fully realized that Joan was still the only really important woman in my life.

Oh, all right. You can't have a head that beautiful nestling in the middle of your chest without feeling a certain…well, a quickening of your pulse, at least. It can happen even in the presence of death, when you've just been shaken to the depths in a ghastly way. Perhaps because of that…

Sex and death. Don't be morbid, Ralphie boy. Don't turn the clock back and let the old Freudian catch-alls of a century ago confuse and mislead you. Half of all that has been made clearer because we know now what Man was like five million years ago when he was a very predatory ape.

Sure, sex and death are closely linked. Dawn man went hunting and slew a cave bear and threw it down before his mate, all bloody, with pride swelling in him and just the excitement of the hunt, the thrill and danger of it, made him want to make love in just as exciting a way.

But sex and life are even more closely linked, and in life there are loyalties to consider and one woman becomes more important to you than all the rest and you don't need that kind of stimulation to enable you to make love to her in the most exciting possible way.

The old stirring is still there, the death-sex linkage, and it can hit you hard at times and you have to keep a tight grip on yourself to keep from succumbing to it. But you can do it if you try.

Of course I was being unfair to her. The sex-death linkage had no more relation to the glow I'd felt back in the lakeside tavern than it did now to her as an individual. I'd have felt the same stirring if I'd been guiding Joan out of the Chart Room with her head on my breast—more of a stirring because Joan was the one woman in the world for me.

What it really meant was that the woman with the hair piled up high on her head filled me with a two-way sense of guilt. The life-sex linkage was better than the death-sex linkage, and the one and only woman feeling better than the promiscuous amorousness that any beautiful woman can arouse in the male. And right at the moment she represented both of the more primitive aspects of sex.

But the dice had just fallen that way. It wasn't her fault and now she was close to hysteria and needed reassurance and all the comfort I could give her.

As soon as we were out in the passageway I asked her to tell me who she was. Her name. So much had happened between us that it seemed unbelievable that I still didn't know that much about her.

"I thought I told you right after we left the spaceport," she said. "I thought you knew. It's Helen…Helen Barclay."

So...the old wonder name, the magical name, the Topless Towers of Illium name. How often it seemed to go with her kind of woman. How could she have been Margaret or Janice or Barbara...attractive as those names were. Lilith perhaps...yes. Or Eva...because I've often felt that Eve must have been a woman of glamour, red-headed and with a temper a little on the fiery side, because how else could she have come down to us as Earth's first legendary temptress? But otherwise...Helen, the glamour name that led the list.

Why was I letting my mind go off at such an absurd tangent, when right ahead of me the stern-obligation stream I've mentioned was widening out, filling with rapids, becoming a river which could have swallowed up the sky ship, or wrecked it...if I failed to take up a giant's stance right in the middle of it. Wade in and thrust the waters aside, Ralphie boy. It's your duty. Try to think of yourself as a giant.

What made it tough was...I didn't feel at all like a giant. But what had just happened in the Chart Room couldn't be ignored. A lot of questions would have to be asked fast, and if the explanations sounded like lies, if Helen Barclay refused to cooperate, some very drastic action might have to be taken. I hoped she didn't have anything ugly to conceal. Just the thought was hateful to me, because I believed in her and trusted her. But the way I felt had nothing to do with an obligation I had no right to sidestep for as short a distance as the width of an electron-microscoped virus.

I was glad that I wouldn't have to do the questioning. Not straight off, anyway—not until I knew much more than I did, and all of the big, vital questions had been answered with candor and I could go right on feeling the way I did about her with a clear conscience. I hoped to God it would be with candor. If someone is dying and you can do nothing to save him and what he's done or hasn't done is of no importance to anyone but himself…you don't ply him with questions. But what she'd done or hadn't done could send the sky ship down into the gulfs in flaming ruin, because all of the passengers are encased in a fragile kind of bubble and the slightest pinprick could puncture it.

The pinprick, for instance, of an Earthside conspirator, traveling along with the bubble out into space and awaiting just the right moment to insert the tiny, darkly gleaming point of the pin under the skin of the bubble.

And she wasn't dying, but alive—and could, if she had nothing to conceal, have no trouble in convincing the commander of the sky ship that any such fear was groundless.

I had to take her straight to the Commander. Otherwise I'd have to take it up with someone of lesser authority and show him the insignia and question her myself in private. I couldn't see any advantage to doing that. It would leave the corpse in the Chart Room unexplained and the Commander would not take kindly to having anything as disturbing as that left lying around in a loose-end way for him to worry about.

It would mean, of course, that I would have to show him the insignia. That was the bad part, the one thing I wanted most to avoid. But I could see no effective way of avoiding it now, because he was, after all, in command of the sky ship and directly responsible for its safety. He had every right to be the first to question her, unless I chose to supplant that right with what the insignia represented. To do so would not have been wise for a dozen reasons, the chief one being that when a man is in a firm position to exercise reasonably high authority it's always a mistake to go over his head unless you're sure you can make a better job of it than he could, despite his specialized knowledge. I didn't think for a moment I could come anywhere near equaling Commander Littlefield's competence in guarding the safety of a Mars' rocket...so to curtail his authority in a high-handed way would have been worse than inexcusable.

But I would still have to show him the insignia...or I would not be permitted to sit in on the questioning.

We were at the end of the passageway now and just by making a sharp left turn I could have taken her into the cabin section and introduced her to Joan. Perhaps, out of compassion, I should have done that...let her relax in a lounge chair and look out at the cool, untroubled stars, and regain a little more of her composure. Some of it was coming back, she wasn't trembling as violently now, and women seem to know better than men how to ease shock-engendered agitation...especially when it's another woman they have to soothe and sympathize with. I could trust Joan to handle it like an expert. "Of course, you poor darling. I know just how you feel. Ralph will know what to do. Don't think about it. Just stay right here with us until Ralph comes back."

It would have been the kind thing to do, all right. For an instant I hesitated and almost committed an act of madness.

When you've something to conceal, it's much easier to avoid a thoughtless admission, a damaging slip of the tongue, when you've had time to collect your thoughts and decide in advance exactly how much of the truth it's wise to reveal. She was too agitated now to guard against slips and our chances of getting at the truth would be much better. And like the short-on-brains, over-chivalrous lug I could be on rare occasions—I hoped they were rare—I'd almost torn it.


## CHAPTER EIGHT


UNLIKE JONATHAN TRILLING, COMMANDER Littlefield was the kind of man who was what he was in an uncomplicated way. You didn't have to try to analyze why he impressed you as he did, because it was all there on display, right out in the open. He was big and robust looking, with a granite-firm jaw and the kind of features that take a long time to develop the lines of character that are etched into them, because a man who has his emotions well under control in his youth will pass into middle-age before you can tell from his expression just how much maturity and strength resides in him.

There are bland-faced lads who seem to have no lines of character at all in their countenances up to about the age of twenty-eight. But when you hear them talk you change your mind very quickly about them, and when they are forty-five the lines are all there, deeply-etched, and the mystery is explained. Commander Littlefield was that kind of man.

We had several very serious things to discuss, because five hours had passed since I'd sat facing him in the same chair and Helen Barclay had sat in another chair at right angles to a third chair, which he had drawn out from his desk and occupied for a full hour without a coffee break, his eyes searching her face as she talked. His stare was a kind of interrogation in itself, and it must have been hard for her to endure. I think it would have angered me a little, if I hadn't suspected what was behind it.

Her story stood up very well and had the ring of truth and her eyes never wavered. But he was hoping they would, then he could detect in her eyes a flicker of hesitation, of evasiveness, which would give her away.

But he hadn't. Her story had stood up almost *too* well...because the truth always has a few flaws and inconsistencies in it. Memory is never a perfect enough mirror to permit anyone to avoid contradictions when they are doing their best to tell nothing but the truth, even under oath.

But she hadn't seemed to be lying, and in the end I think she convinced him completely, because toward the end he stopped looking at her as if every word she said was impressing him unfavorably.

And now she was in the sick bay, recovering from shock, and I was back again for another talk with the Commander.

He began by saying: "I don't know just how I should address you, Mr. Graham—sir. That silver hawk gives you a Colonization Board clearance that's a little on the special side...you'll have to admit. The first man who wore it got a little angry when anyone addressed him as 'General' because that's a strictly military title, and military titles haven't been in common use for forty years. There's not supposed to be any army anymore—on Earth or on Mars. But I've always sort of liked 'General' and that insignia is practically the equivalent of five stars."

"I'm afraid I don't like 'General' at all," I said. "The title is...Ralph."

"Well...suit yourself. *Ralph*. I'm a simple soldier at heart, I suppose—always will be, even though I hold the rank of Commander. You're young enough to be my son, so that informal crap doesn't go too much against the grain, if you're that serious about it."

"I'm serious about it," I said. "And you're not old enough to be my father. An older brother, perhaps. You can't stretch it any further than that."

"What do you mean I can't? I'm an old man of forty-eight. Hair thinning, going a little to fat. My God, a Wendel Atomics or Endicott Fuel top executive couldn't look any older, and they've got a head start on the rest of us. They start burning out at thirty-five."

"There's not an ounce of fat on you, as far as I can see," I assured him.

"That's going to handicap you on Mars, Ralph. Eyesight not what it should be in a five-star general. Look again, look closer. I've got a pot belly you'd notice, all right, if I didn't exercise to keep it down."

I'd skipped over his reference to Wendel Atomics and Endicott, maybe subconsciously, but it must have registered belatedly in a very pronounced way, because something in my expression turned him dead serious in an instant. No man ever speaks with complete levity about his age, but what there was of ironic amusement in his gray eyes vanished and his lips tightened.

"Well…suppose we go over what we've got," he said. "I'll be grateful for any ideas, any suggestions you may care to make. I've found out something that's going to give you a jolt. It may even rock you back on your heels, depending on how easily you can be rocked. But it will keep…until we've discussed what she told us. What do you think of her story?"

"I believe it," I said. I didn't think it was necessary to elaborate.

"Well…I'm afraid I do too, more's the pity. If I thought she was lying I'd have more of a lever to pry what we don't know loose."

There was a thin sheet of paper covered with very fine handwriting on his desk. He picked it up and ran his eyes over it.

"I sort of summarized what she told us," he said. "But there's no sense in your reading this. I can summarize it even more briefly by skipping two-thirds of what I have here."

"You might as well," I told him. "She talked and I listened for at least twenty minutes. Then we both questioned her. In a question-and-answer session like that the vital points are apt to get a little blurred."

"Well, we know she did something no one has ever done before—stowed away on a Mars' ship. I'd have said it

69

couldn't be done...and so would you, I'm sure, because you're as familiar with the inspection routine as I am. You passed through it. No one could possibly get inside a Mars' rocket without a Board clearance and a personal, ten-point identification check every step of the way. In other words, you can't just ascend the launching pad, be whisked up to the passenger section and walk right in. There's only one way you can get inside without passing the four inspection points, with machines X-raying you from head to toe."

"I know," I said. "It was a damn clever stunt."

"It was more than a stunt. It was an achievement on the creative genius level. It took planning and foresight. And...luck. A great deal of luck. But that doesn't detract from the brilliance of it. She found out that we were installing a new cybernetic robot, to replace one that had developed electronic fatigue and had to be removed for repairs and a long rest. And she knew that we wouldn't X-ray a robot or subject it to any of the usual tests. It would just be wheeled right in."

Littlefield paused an instant, then went on. "She knew there was plenty of room inside a cybernetic robot that large, between the tiers of memory banks and all the other gadgetry, for the carrying out of what she had in mind—a stowaway gamble that was almost sure to succeed. She provided for her comfort during the long trip in half-dozen ingenious ways, as we know, and made sure that the food concentrates she took along were high in essential proteins.

"She knew, of course, that she couldn't stay inside the robot without coming out at all. She'd have to emerge occasionally, if only to ease the psychological strain. But she used good judgment and only emerged when she was absolutely sure that it would be safe."

"But once she didn't," I said.

"Once she didn't. Once she felt she couldn't stand the tensions that were building up in her any longer and she took a chance and came out when she wasn't sure the Chart Room would be deserted. You told me you thought it was never left unguarded. Well…that isn't strictly true. There's a built-in security alert system in all of the robots and we can risk leaving it unguarded for a few minutes, when every member of the crew is needed elsewhere, to take care of some particularly troublesome space headache. That's what we call the small and seldom very serious emergencies which are always arising in a sky ship this large."

"But if she heard someone moving about…she must have been crazy to emerge," I said.

"That's just it. She wasn't sure she heard anyone. In fact, she was almost sure it would be safe to emerge. She'd learned to trust her instincts, and the silence was almost unbroken. Just once she thought she heard a slight sound, but she put it down to the tension that was building up in her. She felt she *had* to emerge."

"And he caught her," I said, nodding. "And was more enraged than he had any right to be. His fury was maniacal. If you'd seen the look on his face and the way he was twisting her wrist you'd have been sure as I was that he was quite capable of killing her. And that's the most puzzling part of it. We can't explain it—and neither can she. That's the one part of her story I was afraid you wouldn't believe."

"I didn't for a moment," Littlefield said. "I was sure she was lying…until the look of bewilderment in her eyes convinced me she was telling the truth."

"You didn't want to talk about him until you'd examined the body," I said. "I guess I got a little angry when you were so damned insistent on that point. I was just about to—well, use that silver bird to make you change your mind. That used to be called 'pulling rank' on someone you respect and who

has every right to tell you off. Since you like to play soldier—
and I mean that in a complimentary way—you're free to go
ahead and tell me off now, if you want to."

"Hell no. You had every right to press me. I just felt a
little guilty and ashamed, I guess—to think that I'd let a
crewman come aboard this sky ship who had managed in
some way to deceive the Board. I was pretty sure, even then,
that his clearance papers must have been forged, but I wanted
a chance to examine the body before I committed myself, one
way or the other."

"I guess I'd have done the same," I said.

"Yes... Well, I'd have gone right down to the Chart Room
and examined the body before I listened to what she had to
say...if you hadn't given me some very sound advice. If we
questioned her while she was in a keyed up state we'd have a
better chance of getting at the truth."

I'd almost tripped over that one myself, so I didn't rate the
compliment he was paying me. But it was too minor to make
me feel conscience-bound to disillusion him.

"You saw me click the officer-section communicator on
and talk into it for a minute or two," he went on. "I ordered
a double guard posted in the Chart Room, but I told them
not to touch the body until I had a chance to get down there
myself. It's just as well I did, because something was found
on the body I wouldn't have wanted anyone else to see."

He was smiling a little and I wondered why, until he
exploded the bombshell—the thing he'd said would rock me
back on my heels.

"He'd deceived the Board with a vengeance, apparently.
There was a sealed envelope on him and when I tore it open
there was a card in it. It wasn't a Board clearance card. It
was a Wendel Atomics private police card and it identified
him as the kind of secret agent you'd trade in for a snake if
you *had* to have something poisonous on board and were

given a free choice in the matter. The Wendel police are little better than hired killers—although perhaps a few of them are generous-minded enough to feel that when you've beaten a man insensible it's going a little too far to put a bullet in him as well. And the Wendel secret agents are the worst sadists of the lot. They're hand-picked for shrewdness and when you get intelligence along with brutality there's no refinement of cruelty that won't be resorted to when the going gets rough."

"Good God!" I said. "So that's why—No...no. It doesn't quite explain why just the sight of Helen Barclay emerging from the robot enraged him the way it did. Just the fact that there was a woman stowaway on Board shouldn't have angered him at all. It wasn't his headache, because he was merely masquerading as a crewman. Even a man who felt some responsibility in the matter would have only been a little angered."

Littlefield nodded. "Don't think that hasn't occurred to me. If he'd never set eyes on her before, or had no idea who she was...it's hard to see why he should have become enraged, as you say. That's why I've gone to such lengths to make sure she was telling us the full truth when she explained why getting to Mars was so important to her."

He didn't have to read from the paper he was still holding to help me recall in detail everything she'd said during that part of the question-and-answer session. It had made too deep an impression on me. It had also struck a vital nerve, because it was tied in with my assignment. Not directly, because I could have completed my big job without so much as talking to her again. But she was going to Mars because of something that Wendel Atomics had done.

Wendel Atomics was the exposed nerve, because anything that had to do with the Martian power combines was of vital interest to me, if only on the general information level.

In her case it was a personal matter, just between Wendel and herself. A very small matter to Wendel but overwhelmingly important to her.

Her brother, an electronic engineer, was dying by inches in a Wendel laboratory. Slow, radioactive poisoning meant very little to Wendel Atomics apparently, when just one small human cog was afflicted with it and they still needed his services.

So she had used her own knowledge of electronics and a very great resourcefulness and a high I.Q. to stowaway in a cybernetic robot and was on her way to Mars to see what a woman of courage, entirely alone, could do to save the life of the only brother she had.

She had tried to get a clearance from the Board and failed and that explained how she happened to be in the New Chicago spaceport bar when my own life had been in even more immediate danger...because slow, radioactive poisoning takes a long time to kill and if you can stop it in time there's always a chance that the victim will recover.

"I've been checking up ever since you left," Littlefield was saying. "I managed to get through to Earth on the needle frequencies and Trilling knows now that you showed me the silver bird. The code I used to tell him that was too complicated to be broken by the big-brained inhabitants of Alpha Centauri's third planet, if—as seems unlikely—such a planet exists."

"And you didn't even tell me," I said. "I suppose I should be burned up about it."

"No, you shouldn't be. I just saved you a lot of unnecessary explaining. You can talk to Trilling all you want to from here on in, but I've cushioned the shock for you, taken a little of the edge off the way he seemed to feel for a minute or two."

"Well...all right," I said. "Just what did you tell him."

"I asked him to do what he could to confirm her story. So far everything she told us seems to check out. Of course, they haven't been able to turn up too much, and she could still be lying. But we may get more on it later on. Don't count on it, though. I may not even be able to contact Trilling again. The needle frequencies are as unreliable as hell, as you know."

"But you just said I could talk to Trilling myself—"

"If we're lucky. You can't express yourself with precision when you're as troubled as I am right now."

I was troubled too...perhaps more than he was. But just trying to make that concern dwindle a little by turning all the knobs on and off kept me from thinking about it.

"Well...he could have recognized her," I said. "There could have been a link there, since he was a Wendel secret agent and her brother works for Wendel. Maybe they sent him her brother's photograph over the needle frequencies and said: 'Look around for a girl who resembles this man and keep an eye on her. She's one little girl we're worried about.'"

"Oh, sure, that could be it."

"It wouldn't sound quite so ludicrous, Commander, if it was her photograph they managed somehow to send him. Maybe they secured one from her brother without his knowing about it. But still—it wouldn't make much sense. Why should they fear her enough to put a secret agent on her trail? One helpless woman forty million miles from Mars. He couldn't have known she'd smuggle herself on board the rocket in a cybernetic robot...because his rage when he discovered her precluded that. And why would he make the trip if he was out to get her and, for all he knew to the contrary, she was still somewhere in New Chicago?"

"If he was trailing her he could have suspected she might be on board and may have been searching everywhere for her," Littlefield pointed out. "That would even explain his rage when he finally got his hands on her, if we remember the kind of sadistic human animal he was. Frustration alone could produce a rage as violent as that in a Wendel agent—days and nights of fruitless searching. But...I agree with you that it doesn't make sense otherwise. The stumbling block, as you say, is the difficulty in imagining how Wendel Atomics could possibly regard her as that serious a menace. Or fear her at all, for that matter."

That was as far as we got. The officer-section communication instrument on Littlefield's desk started buzzing and he swung about to pick it up, with an almost joyful eagerness.

I was sure that at any other time he'd have accepted that call with no visible display of emotion, just as a routine necessity. But when you've reached a stone wall in a discussion of vital importance and the odds against your making any further progress seem insurmountable, for the moment at least, practically any interruption will be as welcome as sunlight after a drenching rain or a pea-soup fog. It's certainly better than beating your head against stone.

He listened for perhaps ten seconds with the instrument pressed to his ear, with no pronounced change of expression. Then his face blanched and a look of horror came into his eyes.

He slammed the instrument down and headed for the door on the run, completely unmindful of his dignity. Then he seemed to remember that he owed me an explanation—a man of principle will usually take a second or two out for that even when his home is in flames—and turned a yard from the door to shout at me.

"Someone got the nose-cone panel open, climbed outside and is crawling along the airframe toward the jet section! He's wearing magnetic boots and if I'm not mistaken he's equipped with everything he needs to blow the rocket apart."

When he saw the look on my face he added reassuringly. "We've still got a good chance of stopping him in time, because he just climbed out. But we'll have to bring most of the airframe into sharp focus on the viewplate, and pinpoint his every movement."

It came as such a shock to me that I felt I had a good chance of suffocating, just from the way my throat tightened up and my heart started pumping blood at twice its usual rate.

I'm not quite sure how I managed to follow him at a distance of not more than fifteen feet, down three intership ladders and along four branching passageways, without once stopping to get my breath back. I doubt if I could have done that anyway.

Right foot, then left, right left, right left, Ralphie boy, and don't give up the ship. Never give up the ship when there's a chance to save it. There's nothing painful about being vaporized in space. Remember that, keep it firmly in mind. Nothing painful, nothing sad…just a quick end to all you've had.

I don't know why I thought the Chart Room looked deserted, like a big, unoccupied mausoleum with tiers for coffins—dozens of coffins—running up both of its sides. No coffins yet, just the empty shelves, for burial time had not yet arrived. But how could the Chart Room have looked deserted, when it wasn't at all?

There were a dozen officers standing in front of the big lighted screen and when we crossed the room to join them without announcing our arrival—well, that made fourteen.

I can't even explain how I got the idea there was a chill in the air that seemed to wrap itself around me in moist, clinging folds, because no section of the sky ship was more comfortably heated.

I didn't spend more than a minute or two trying to puzzle it out, because the "furious sick shapes of nightmare," to quote from a poem I wasn't sure I'd ever read, only disturb you when you give them more encouragement than they're entitled to.

The only really important thing was that we could see him in bent light on the big screen—a tiny, spacesuited figure climbing along the airframe, laden down with something cumbersome that he kept pushing before him in a completely weightless way as he inched further and further toward the rocket's stern.

All at once, I knew what was going to happen to him. I was as sure of it as I am that I have two big toes that point a little inward and that Joan sometimes tenderly jokes about.

Between Earth and Mars space isn't empty. It hasn't been empty for more than half a century, which is a pretty good record on the survival scale for man-made, mechanical implants. The early Sputniks didn't last one-tenth as long.

I knew without waiting for Commander Littlefield to finish what he was saying to one of the officers and issue a command that the needle frequencies scattered throughout the void on all sides of us were the only composite weapon we could count on to save the sky ship and all the people between its decks who didn't want to be vaporized. And that took in practically everyone on board.

Sure, I know. Everyone had thought that the millions of filament-thin wires which had been put into orbit around Earth in the seventh and eighth decades of the twentieth century and later into orbit around Mars and far out into interstellar space would only be used for purposes of communication. Project Needles, or, if you want to be strictly technical, Project West Ford.

God grant that they may some day be used in no other way. But when a man climbs out on the airframe of a sky ship, for the sole purpose of blowing it up—

There is only one way I can do justice to the speed with which it happened and the awful, mind-numbing finality of it. It is not something that should be recorded in a paragraph, a page, but in two sentences at most.

Commander Littlefield issued a command, and a light on the instrument panel blinked, and a million magnetized filaments converged, united and so united, converged again on the airframe of the sky ship. There was a blinding flash of light and the tiny human figure was gone.

The first words Commander Littlefield spoke, after that, were to me.

"Whoever he was, he must have wanted her dead pretty badly...to have been willing to blow up the sky ship and kill himself in the process."

There was a strange look on his face and his gray eyes met mine with a question in them.

Then he spoke the question aloud. "Or was it you, Ralph, whom he had in mind?"

## CHAPTER NINE

THE CLANG OF THE OPENING PORT WAS still ringing in my ears when I walked out of the sky ship with Joan on my arm and looked down over the big metal corkscrew directly beneath me. I knew straight off I'd made a mistake. I should have looked up at the sky instead. I should have squared my shoulders, drawn the crisp, tangy air deep into my lungs and established rapport with Mars more gradually.

A delay, of only a moment or two would have spared me the too sudden shock of finding myself three hundred feet in the air, dazzled by an unexpected brightness, and supported by nothing I'd have cared to trust my weight to on Earth.

We were standing on a thin strip of metal, a mere spider-web tracery, and if I'd lost my balance and gone crashing through the guard rail there would have been no mountaineer's rope to save me. What was worse, I'd have taken Joan with me.

The danger was illusionary, of course…solely in my mind. The underwriters go to a great deal of expense and trouble to make sure there will be no tragic accidents when the big risks have been left behind in space.

The guardrail was chest-high and sturdy enough, and no one had ever gone crashing through it. But you can't reason with a feeling, and for an instant the yawning emptiness beneath me made me feel that I was already past the rail, twisting and turning, flailing the air in a three-hundred-foot plunge.

I was sure that Joan was experiencing the same kind of irrational giddiness, for she drew in her breath sharply and a shiver went through her. A fear of great heights is one phobia that is shared by practically everyone.

The big metal corkscrew beneath us was the landing frame into which the rocket had descended and we were standing high up on that enormous spiral, which curved down and outward like an immense silvery cocoon.

A figure of speech, sure. But not as wide of the mark as most of the images that flash across your mind when you're keyed up abnormally and a lot of new colors, and sights and sounds rush in on you and upset all of your calculations as to how sober-minded you're going to stay. Your grasp on reality slips a little, as if you were holding it right before your eyes like a book, and wearing glasses so strong that the print blurs. You're in a fantasy world of your own creating, seeing things that can't be blamed on whoever wrote the book. A fussy, unimaginative little guy, perhaps, who has spent most of his life within sight of his own doorstep and has never felt the great winds of space blowing cold upon him.

There's a big, night-flying Sphinx moth with death-heads on each of its wings, and there were times when I'd thought of the Mars ship as not so different from that kind of moth. And now it was as if the sky ship had turned back into a caterpillar again, and spun a cocoon for itself, and was quietly reposing in the pupa stage, its rust-red end vanes folded back, its long length mottled and space-eroded where the atomic jets had seared it.

There was nothing wrong in giving my imagination carte-blanche to go into free fall like that, because when you're standing on a dizzy height staring down at a new world forty million miles from Earth you've got to let the strangeness and bursting wonder of it…along with the dire forebodings…take firm hold of you. Otherwise you won't feel yourself to be a part of it, won't be equipped with what it takes to probe beneath the surface of things in a realistic way and feel like a native son even in the presence of the unknown.

Three hundred feet below me more activity was taking place than I had ever seen crowded into an area of equal size on Earth. Just as a guess, I'd have said that the spaceport's disembarkation section was about six hundred feet square. But right at that moment I had no real stomach for guessing games—only a hollowness where my stomach was supposed to be.

Far below the disembarkation section was in high gear, and the clatter of it, the rushings to and fro, the grinding and screeching of giant cranes, and atomic tractors, and rising platforms crowded to capacity with specialized robots, most of them scissor-thin and all of them operated by remote control…would have half-deafened me if I'd been standing a hundred feet lower down.

Even from the top of the spiral the clamor had to be heard to be believed. But what astounded me most was the newness, brightness, sharply delineated aspect of everything within range of my vision. I could see clear to the edge of the spaceport, and the four other securely berthed rockets stood out with a startling clarity, their nose cones gleaming in the bright Martian sunlight. The big lifting cranes stood out just as sharply, and although the zigzagging tractors looked like painted toys, red and blue and yellow, I would have sworn under oath that not one of them cast a shadow.

The twenty-five or thirty human midgets who were moving in all directions across the field, between machines that seemed too formidable to be trusted had the brittle, sheen-bright look of figures cut out of isinglass.

Another illusion, of course. There had to be shadows, because there was nothing on Mars that could have brought about that big a change in the laws of optics. But by the same token the length and density of shadows can be altered a bit by atmospheric conditions, making light interception turn playful. So I didn't strain my eyes searching for deep purple halos around the human midges.

My only immediate concern was to reassure Joan in a calm and forceful way and escort her safely down to ground level, without letting her suspect that I shared her misgivings as to the stability of the spiral.

It was ridiculous on the face of it. But, as I've said, you can't argue with a feeling that whispers that your remote, dawn age ancestors must have felt the same way when they climbed out on a limb overhanging a precipice, and felt the whole tree begin to sway and shake beneath them.

"Hold tight to the rail and don't look down," I cautioned. "There's no real danger...because a first-rate welding job was done on this structure. Barring an earthquake, it should be just as safe a century from now."

I shot a quick, concerned glance at her along with the warning. I guess I must have thought she'd be more shaken, than she was, for she smiled when she saw the look of surprise in my eyes. It took me half a minute to realize that my guess as to how she'd be taking it hadn't gone so wide of the mark. Her pallor gave her away.

"A century would be much too long to wait," she breathed. "Another five minutes would be too long. If it's going to collapse, I'd rather find out right now."

I nodded and we started down. Several other passengers had emerged from the port and were looking up at the sky or downward as I'd done. Three men and a woman had emerged ahead of us and were almost at the base of the spiral. So far nothing had happened to them.

I've often toyed with the thought that there may be windows in the mind we can see out of sometimes—at oblique angles and around corners and without turning our heads. I could visualize the passengers who were descending behind us more clearly than you usually can in a mind's eye picture. Each face was in sharp focus and there was no blurring of their images as they moved. It was as if I was staring straight up at them through a crystal-clear pane of glass.

In that astonishingly bright inner vision—why look up and back when I did not doubt its accuracy?—Commander Littlefield was wasting no time in setting a good example. He'd descended the spiral so many times that great height meant nothing to him. He'd be ascending and descending at least ten more times just in the next few hours. But this was his big moment. I could already picture him striding across the disembarkation section to the Administration Unit with his shoulders held straight, and announcing officially, with a ring of pride in his voice, that the trip had been completed in record time, and the rocket had been berthed successfully.

He was descending now with a confident smile on his lips, his Mars' legs buoyantly supporting him.

Behind him came the small group who had been closest to us in space. They were doing their best to stay calm, but there was a slight flicker of apprehension in their eyes. Our section had been the first to disembark, because Littlefield had agreed with me that it might have seemed a little strange if I'd been accorded that privilege and it had been denied to the others. Why give anyone who might have outwitted every screening precaution the idea that I might be a man apart, with so big a job awaiting me on Mars that getting started on it without delay was damned important to me. It was natural enough for one or two sections to be cleared fast and emerge with the Commander. But others would have to await their turn in line and quarantine checkups could drag along for hours.

"It's funny how long it takes to get even a little lower when you're this high up," Joan said, her fingers tightening on my arm. "We're not anything like as high as when we started. But nothing down below looks any larger."

"We're not a fourth of the way down, and the human eye is a very poor judge of distances," I said, reassuringly. "It would be better if you let go of my arm and just kept your right hand on the rail. We sway more this way."

"When you look down from the observation roof of the North-Western University Building you can see all of New Chicago, and practically half of Lake Michigan," she complained breathlessly. "But it never made me feel as giddy as this."

"You had a firmer support under you," I said. "But not a safer one. There's no danger at all. You can be absolutely sure of that. What could happen to us?"

It was one of those silly questions you sometimes ask when you want to reassure someone you're a little concerned about. But a silly question can sometimes be answered in a totally unexpected way—suddenly, terribly and with explosive violence. It can be answered by a voice of thunder out of the sky, or a wild, savage cry in the night, or in a quieter way, but with just as terrifying an outcome. There are a hundred cataclysms of nature, which can give the lie to what you thought was only a silliness.

No matter where you are or how secure you feel, never ask what could happen in a world where nothing is sure, where no one is ever completely safe. Death is death. From end to end of his big estate may be a lifetime's journey for some men. But he can cover the distance with the speed of light, because Death is one space traveler—the only one—who knows exactly how to outdistance light.

Even if you're alone in a steel-walled vault it's a dangerous question to ask. It's ten times as dangerous when you're descending a swaying metal corkscrew forty million miles from Earth and there may be someone eighty feet above you who has failed twice as Death's emissary and would be covered with shame if it happened again.

I felt hardly anything for an instant when the dart sliced deep into the soft flesh between my shoulder blades. I didn't even know it was a dart and kept right on walking. It was as if a bee had stung me—a tired bee who couldn't sting very hard. There was just a little stab of pain, a burning sensation that lasted less than a second.

I felt it, all right. But it didn't startle me enough to stop me dead in my tracks. A thing like that seldom does, if you're moving steadily forward. It takes a second or two after you've felt the pain for the implications to dawn on you.

When they did the pain was back, and this time it was excruciating. My whole shoulder was laced with fire, as if a red-hot iron had been laid against it. If right at that moment I'd smelled an odor of burning flesh I'd have been sure there could be no other explanation, despite its transparent absurdity.

Even then I kept right on walking. I staggered a little but I bit down hard on my underlip to avoid crying out. I didn't want to alarm Joan until I was sure. It could still have been just a very severe muscular spasm—the kind of agonizing cramp that can hit you in the leg sometimes in the middle of the night, so that you awake out of a deep sleep bathed in cold sweat, and with your teeth chattering.

That was what seemed to be happening now. My teeth started chattering and I could feel sweat oozing out all over me. There was only one difference. The pain was in my shoulder, not my leg, and it wasn't easing up the way spasm pain does after a minute or two. It couldn't have gotten worse, because it had been excruciating from the beginning. But other things started getting worse fast. The burning sensation spread to my lungs and my throat muscles started constricting, so that every breath I drew was an agony.

I couldn't pretend any longer, and I didn't try to. I went down on my knees, clutching at my chest and swaying back against the rail. I suppose I must have groaned or made some sort of sound, because Joan swung about and was kneeling beside me in an instant, her face ashen.

I must have looked terrible, or all of the color would not have drained out of her face so fast, or her eyes gone quite so wide with alarm.

I made a half-hearted try at straightening up, but only succeeded in bringing my collapse closer to zero-count by sagging more heavily back against the rail.

"Darling, what is it? *Tell me!*" Her voice was demanding, wildly insistent. "Please...I've got to know. If it's your heart—"

I shook my head. I went through a kind of little death just trying to get a few words out. "Something struck me…in the back. See…what it is. Feel around with your hand."

"All right, darling. Just don't move. No—you'll have to lift yourself up a little more. Try, darling. Your back's right against the rail."

I did more than try. I helped her by gritting my teeth and flopping over on my stomach. But the pain that lanced through my chest made me almost black out for an instant.

There was a clamor above us now, and I thought I heard Littlefield's voice raised in a shout, followed by a scream of terror. Possibly someone had seen me slump and jumped to the conclusion that the spiral was collapsing.

There was no chance of that, so I couldn't have cared less how close to panic the people up above were. Right at the moment it didn't concern me. I was only concerned with what Joan might find when her fingers started probing. If a bullet had ploughed into me and her fingers came away wetly red I'd know for sure whether it was as bad as I feared. It helps to know, when there's a tormenting uncertainty in your mind along with the physical pain.

I could feel her hand fumbling with my shirt, getting it loosened. Then they were moving up, down and across my back. Cautiously, gently, with the nurselike competence which women usually manage to summon to their aid in an emergency, no matter how shaken they are.

After a moment her fingers stopped moving and she drew in her breath sharply.

Being in agony and on the verge of blacking out carries with it a penalty. You can't always hear what someone close to you may be saying, even when it's of life-and-death importance.

I caught a few words, however, just enough to know it was a dart before I lost consciousness. And her look told me what kind of dart it was.

Or maybe it wasn't her look, just what I knew about darts in general. The kind of dart that's in common use today as a weapon is quite unlike the primitive blowgun darts of South American Indians a century ago. Science, like everything else, progresses, especially in the field of weapons. The modern dart is just as simple, in a way, but you take it out of a wafer-thin metal case as you would a hypodermic needle and you fit the three parts very carefully together and you use a liquid propellant to blow it out of a very slender tube of gleaming metal. And there's space in it for poison.

It's handier, tidier than the small robot killers with their intricate internal gadgetry, even though it requires precision aiming and you're much more likely to be observed while you're taking aim, and be compelled to pay the customary penalty for murder.

I'd managed to roll back on my side, and lying then in agony, trying to catch what Joan was saying, sort of telescoped all that for me, so that it registered in my mind in a more rapid way than it does when you're trying to explain it academically. Everything I knew about darts came sweeping into my mind, and I remembered something else that helped to explain the agony.

The modern dart changes shape the instant it enters a man's body, opening up like a pair of six-bladed scissors, cutting, slashing, severing veins and muscles and nerve ganglions. And if it strikes an artery—

It doesn't even have to be a poisoned dart to kill a man. The feathered part remains in the wound, only slightly embedded. But if you have any sense you resist an impulse to pull it out, because when you do that it's very difficult to stop the bleeding. It's a job for a skilled surgeon and Joan's look told me that there was no time to be lost. The wisest thing I could do was to put my complete trust in Commander Littlefield. The quicker he got one of the passengers or a crewman to help him carry me down to ground level and bundle me into an ambulance the better my chances would be.

Joan seemed to be one jump ahead of me, for she leapt up quickly and started back up the spiral. She didn't even press my hand in reassurance, but that was all right with me. I knew why she hadn't. Every second counted, and she loved me too much to be anything but firmly practical about it.

I remember thinking, just before I blacked out, *how adequate are the hospital facilities here? And what about the surgeons? Oh God, what if they are fifth-raters, what if the hospital is understaffed? What if they bungle it, but good?*

When you black out and stay blacked out for a long period, questions like that lose most of their tormenting aspects. You may still feel emotionally disturbed by them, when the darkness lifts a little and you remember having asked yourself questions someone somewhere should have answered—if you'd only stayed around long enough to make a lot of friends and influence people and make them eager to oblige you in every possible way. But it isn't too disturbing, because you can't even remember what the questions were.

The trouble was...I didn't stay blacked out. Not completely. I woke up at intervals and heard snatches of conversation and I even saw—the Mars Colony.

I saw quite a bit of the Colony before they eased me down in a hospital bed, and covered me with warm blankets and I blacked out again.

I saw the streets I'd traveled forty million miles to visit, and the people I'd come to make friends with, and the kids in their space helmets, looking precisely as they did on Earth. (What further frontier did they hope to explore...Alpha

Centauri or just one of the giant outer planets?) I saw the prefabricated metal buildings, four, eight and twenty stories high, with their slanting roofs, rust-red and verdigris-green blue in the early morning sunlight and the stores that were all glass and the strange looking supermarkets with their almost cathedral-like domes. And just for good measure, eight or ten bar-flanked streets with big parking lots where the bars gave way to barracks that straggled out into the desert and had a primitive, twentieth century, shanty-town look.

There were people everywhere, but when you're propped up on a cot in a speeding ambulance you can't tell whether the people who go flying past look just the way people do on Earth, or have a more robust, happier look. Or a more restless and discontented look. It's even hard to tell whether young people or middle-aged people predominate, or just how many very old people there are. Or how many infants in arms, except that there did seem to be an exceptionally large number of children, either being wheeled or carried or toddling along in the wake of their parents, or playing games with the fierce competitiveness of twelve-year-olds in fenced-in sand lots which no one had taken the trouble to pave.

There were theaters too—places of amusement, anyway—which you could tell featured lively entertainment just from the gaudy blue and yellow posters on their facades.

That there were machines clattering past goes without saying. A tremendous amount of new construction was under way in every part of the Colony and if you just say "Mars" in a word association test one man or woman in three will come right back with "Machinery."

There were pipes, too—huge and branching, big, shining metal tubes that arched above buildings and ran parallel with almost every street in the Colony. A tremendous brood of writhing snakes was what they reminded me of—the artificial kind that kids delight in scaring people with at birthday parties, all mottled over with the bronze sheen of copperheads, but looking more like boa constrictors in their tremendous girth.

Another kind of snake image flashed into my mind as I stared out through the windows of the ambulance at that interlocking power-fuel network. It came swimming right out of the history books I'd poured over in fascination when I was knee-high to a grasshopper. Sure, they were Diamond Back rattlesnakes and the Mars Colony was right out of the Old West of covered wagon and gold-prospecting days.

Of course it wasn't, because the twenty-first century technology had made it completely modern in some respects. But it was like the Old West in a good many other ways. It had the same rugged, mirage-bright pioneer look, as if the desert sands were blowing right into the heart of the colony, swirling about, filling the windy places and the sand lots where the kids were playing with a haze that could just as easily have been gold dust that some careless, giant-size prospector had spilled by accident when he'd brought it in from the hills for weighing.

Actually, there's nothing on Earth or Mars that can completely shatter that cyclic aspect of history. There's nothing so new that you can look at it and say, "There's nothing of the past here. The break is complete and the past is gone forever and can never return again."

It's just not true. The past does return, shining brightly beneath the bold new pattern, the daring new way of life that Man likes to think he has chiseled from a block of marble that human hands have never touched or human eyes rested upon before.

There's no such block of marble in all the universe of stars. Not really, because what Man can visualize he has already seen and it has become a part of his heritage and the past of that heritage goes flowing into it and he starts off with a veined monolith that is brimming over with human memory patterns, with not a few buried deep in the stone.

But I've forgotten to mention the most important aspect of everything I saw through the windows of that speeding ambulance. It was…the blurred aspect, the way everything kept changing shape and disappearing and pin wheeling at times. It wasn't surprising, because the agony was still with me and I saw everything in fitful starts, in brief flashes, between bouts of blacking out and coming to and blacking out again. But what I did see I saw clearly, with the heightened awareness that often accompanies almost unbearable pain. When white-hot needles of pain are jabbing at your nerves a strange, almost blinding kind of illumination seems to sweep into the brain. But instead of blinding you it makes everything stand out with a startling clarity and you can think clearly too, and even speculate about what you've seen.

It's as if you were caught up in a kind of sharper-than-life dream sequence, or sitting in a darkened theater watching events take place on a dazzlingly bright screen. You may be doubled up with pain, but you keep your eyes on the screen and very little that is happening to the actors and actresses on a dramatic level is lost on you. You even notice small details of background scenery that would escape your attention ordinarily, and exactly what kind of clothes the actresses are wearing. Light summer dresses with plunging necklines or tight-fitting, form-molded swimsuits—things you can't help noticing even when you're doubled up with pain. It's why most of us fight to stay alive, because Nature has made us that way to keep us from letting go of the one thing that makes us stay in the pitcher's box when Death is batting a thousand.

Putting that much stress just on the engendering of life may be a trick and a snare, when Death has set so cruel a trap for the winners, but you seldom hear anyone complaining about it. It takes an awful lot of grief and despair and pain to make anyone angrily resent the sex snare, and take to eulogizing Death instead.

It wasn't the reason everything I saw through the windows of the ambulance registered so sharply in fitful flashes, because I had *that* right at my side. Joan was holding my hand and squeezing it and I only had to turn my head to make me just about the toughest adversary Death ever had. But what I said about the lighted cinema screen still holds. What I did see, I saw with eyes that missed very little. And between the bouts of blacking out the snatches of conversation I overheard came to me just as distinctly.

Part of the time it was a woman's voice I heard and I knew it had to be Joan's voice, because there was no other woman in the ambulance with me. But she wasn't talking to me. She was talking to one of the two men in white who were sitting opposite me. They seemed about a half-mile away most of the time, but occasionally the long bench they were sitting on floated a little closer.

The conversation, as I've said, came to me in snatches and it could hardly have been called a running dialogue. The continuity alone would have gotten a professional scriptwriter fired, no matter how brilliant he was otherwise.

The only way I can whip it into shape is by recording it as if it were continuous, filling in the part I overheard between blackouts with what I didn't hear—staying close enough to what was probably being said to keep the script writer on the job and eating.

I'm pretty sure this is a fairly accurate re-write.

Joan: What kind of a hospital is it? I'm sorry, I... I guess I shouldn't have asked you that. You're on the staff. No matter how frank you might want to be...

Doctor Mile-Away: If I thought it wasn't a good hospital I wouldn't say so, naturally. But it happens to match up very well with the eight or ten you'd want him to be taken to Earthside, if you had a choice. The facilities are first-rate, completely up to date. There are four surgeons I'd trust my life to with equal confidence...and one of them happens to be my dad.

Joan: I hope to God he gets one of them.

Doctor: There are only four surgeons. We don't get too many surgical cases in the Colony—not nearly as many as you might think. There's as much violence here, perhaps, as there is in New Chicago but it takes a different form. We can't keep atomic handguns out of criminal hands as easily as you can in New Chicago, because the lawless element in the Colony has more socio-political power and can get more weapons in that destructive category smuggled in. As you know, an atomic handgun has a very limited destructive potential, since there's no fallout and it can only kill a man standing directly in its path. But when it does...there isn't much margin left for surgery."

Joan: You mean *criminals* are in control here?

Doctor: Oh, it's not quite that bad. Possibly about one colonist in twenty has dangerous criminal tendencies. The proportion is larger here only because it's a new society, with a pioneering outlook. You might call it a wolf-eat-wolf society. On Earth the dog-eat-dog tendencies will probably never be completely eradicated but we've gone a long way in that respect just in the last half-century. Here we have further to go, because the dogs are still wolves.

Joan: Will you ever tame them? My husband may be dying right here; that doesn't look so tame! I think your Mars Colony is a filthy jungle!

Doctor: I didn't have much time to talk with Commander Littlefield. But from what *he* said I'm pretty sure you don't really feel that way. I don't know why you and your husband are here, but the Colonization Board seldom gives clearance to people who feel that way about the future of the Colony. In fact…I can't remember ever having met a man or woman who managed to deceive the Board, because the screening is the opposite of superficial. They go into your past history, I understand, and give you psychological tests I'm not even sure I could pass, convinced as I am that the Colony is still Man's best hope in a world where to stand still is always disastrous. There's no other sane solution to the population problem, just to mention one of the fifty or sixty major problems we'll have to solve or perish in, in the next two centuries. I have my moments of doubt and cynicism…

Joan: You should be having one right now. How would *you* feel if you were taking your wife to the hospital for an emergency operation and didn't know whether she was going to live or die? Suppose it was your wife instead of my husband? We didn't even have time to set foot in the Colony. If there's that much danger before you even—

Doctor: Just hold on a minute. Let's get this straightened out right now. It will make you feel better. No one in the Colony tried to kill your husband. That dart was aimed at him from above—by one of the passengers. They're all being held for questioning and if the firing mechanism is found on one of them—

That, for me, was the end of the dialogue. But just before I blacked out for the last time I saw a sign high up over one of the buildings. It read: WENDEL ATOMICS.

And I went down into the darkness with that sign flashing in big illuminated letters right in the middle of the darkness. WENDEL ATOMICS. WENDEL. WENDEL ATOMICS. And in much smaller letters, which were not nearly as bright: *Endicott Fuel.*

The big letters growing larger, brighter…the small letters dwindling.

Just as I felt myself to be dwindling…as I passed deeper and deeper into the darkness.

## CHAPTER TEN

"HE'S A BIG MAN," I HEARD A WOMAN'S voice say. "It took every ounce of my strength to lift him. But he had to be moved to the edge of the bed, doctor. The sheets had to be changed."

A whirling in my head, needles darting in and out. I had to strain my ears to catch what another voice was saying in reply. It was a man's voice, but gruff, deep-throated and somehow less distinct than the first voice. Perhaps Gruff Voice was standing further from the bed. Or possibly he didn't want me to hear what he was telling the nurse.

She had to be a nurse, because Gruff Voice wasn't addressing her by name. He wasn't calling her Miss Hadley or Miss Betty Anne Simpson-Cruickshank. He was saying "Nurse this," and "Nurse that" and speaking with crisp authority, as if there was a gulf between a nurse and a doctor which even the kindliest, least hidebound of physicians had no right to ignore.

I rather liked his voice, gruff as it was. He spoke with the air of a man who knew his business, with a kind of restrained sympathy—the "no nonsense" approach. Too much calm self-assurance can be irritating, because it usually goes with the inflated egos of people who think very highly of themselves. But in a doctor you don't object to that sort of thing so much.

"He's waking up," Gruff Voice was saying. "Just let him rest and don't encourage him to talk. No more sedation—he won't need it. Did you take his temperature, Nurse?"

"Just ten minutes ago, Doctor. It's on the chart. I always—"

"Put it down immediately? Who do you think you're kidding, Susan, my love? Once in awhile you put it off, when this kind of emergency case makes you wish you had a dozen pairs of hands. You put if off for fifteen or twenty minutes, when you've no reason to think some white-coated drum major is going to barge in unexpectedly, just to lean on you. Did you ever know me to lean, Susan—heavily or otherwise? You're doing the best you can and it's a very good 'best.' I wish we had more 'bests' like it."

"I do feel...sort of wobbly, Roger. I deserve to be leaned on, because once you start feeling that way you're no longer at peak efficiency and you become nervously over-scrupulous. That's both good and bad, if you know what I mean."

"What did you expect, Susan? I could have had a nurse in here to relieve you hours ago if you hadn't been so stubborn. You've been worrying your cute blonde head off without stopping to rest for sixteen hours, and you never set eyes on the guy before this morning. What is there about some men—"

"It was touch and go, Roger. You said yourself that a little of the poison got into his blood. You told me a tenth of a cc would have been fatal."

"That was when I first looked at the lab analysis and took the gloomiest possible view of his chances. I didn't even know you heard me. Damn it all, Susan. Can't a doctor think out loud without giving his most competent nurse a martyr complex? What is there about him? I'm asking you. If he wasn't married I could perhaps understand it. I could at least make a stab at trying to figure it out. But you've seen his wife. A man with a wife as attractive as she is would have to be even more susceptible than I am to look twice at another woman. That's just another way of saying it couldn't happen."

"I've had two long talks with her, Roger. She loves him so much that if anything happened to him I'm afraid to think what she might do. All alone on Mars, with no close relatives or friends to turn to for help and warmth and comfort. She'd need a lot of support, because there's nothing shallow about her. She's the intense type, very deep in her emotions. I'm that way myself."

"You don't have to tell me," I could hear him saying. "You're the empathy-plus type. It's what makes a good many otherwise sensible women embrace the toughest profession on the list. Hard-boiled, unemotional women make good nurses too. But I prefer the kind of nurse you can't help being. Only…a little moderation even in people who go all out can be a saving grace."

"But don't you see, Roger? It means I can identify with her. I know exactly how terrible the uncertainty must be for her, because if I loved a man that much and lost him I'd probably go right out and kill myself. If you want the full truth…there's probably a little of the male-female absurdity mixed up in it too. It's an absurdity in a situation like this, where it makes no sense. But just the fact that he's a man and I'm a woman—"

"Talk like that will get you nowhere," he said. "I'm too sure of you."

There was a rustling sound and a sudden gasp and I was pretty sure I knew what it meant. He'd taken her into his arms and was kissing her. I don't know why I didn't open my eyes. I was fully awake now, aware of every movement in the room. But I just remained quiet and listened, grateful that the needles had stopped jabbing at my temples and my dizziness was practically gone.

Sometimes when you awake suddenly from a deep sleep your eyes feel glued shut, and it takes an effort just to open them. You let it ride for a moment, while you pull yourself together…especially if it's a nightmare you've just awakened from. There's a kind of pleasure in it.

He was talking again. "I've yet to meet a woman who doesn't think that clinical self-analysis will keep a man guessing about her. But that kind of candor will get you nowhere with me, kiddo. I know you too well. Are you convinced?"

"Yes," she said, with a meekness that surprised me. He didn't say anything for a moment, but I could hear him moving about and a metallic click, as if he were folding up his stethoscope or returning a hypodermic to its case.

A sound like that is always a little unnerving and an operating table and a long row of gleaming instruments flashed evanescently across my mind. I wondered how bad it was and if Martian hospitals were well equipped, and had just the right facilities to take care of an emergency case requiring major surgery.

But he'd said I was out of danger, hadn't he…that I didn't even need more sedation? Sure he had. I'd been stabbed with a poisoned dart, but that didn't mean I'd have to go on the operating table. They would never have let the dart stay inside me. If an operation had been needed, it would have been performed immediately…

Perhaps it had. Well, to hell with it. I was out of danger now and beginning to mend and that was the only thing that counted. It had been touch and go, she'd said. And Joan loved me so much that…

Hold on tight to that, Ralphie boy. It's the best news you'll ever hear, even though you knew it all along, were sure of it on the day you married her. What they didn't know and would have to guess about was the feeling of oneness we had whenever we were together.

I let that ride too, sweet as it was to dwell upon, and thought about how mistaken I'd been about the doctor. He wasn't the kind of guy I'd thought him. The "nurse this, nurse that" talk had been either a performance, put on for my benefit just in case I was a little more than semiconscious or—a routine, quickly dropped formality.

The second supposition seemed the most likely. A kind of ritual they went through from habit, and because it's more ethical to keep a doctor-nurse relationship on a formal plane when the patient is under clinical scrutiny. After that, they could relax and be human.

I had no complaint, because I liked both aspects of Gruff Voice's personality. That I liked the nurse goes without saying, not only because of what she'd said about Joan, but because of a certain something...

All right. Gruff Voice had said that he was susceptible beyond the average and so was I. A sweet soft woman bending over you, denying herself sleep just to make sure you'll stay alive, doing her best to ease your pain, sort of...does things to you. It had nothing to do with the way I felt about Joan. It wasn't actual disloyalty...didn't come within a mile of disloyalty. It was just the man-woman absurdity she'd mentioned, only...it wasn't an absurdity and never had been.

It may be a hard thing for a woman to understand, sometimes. But it's never hard for a man to understand, if he's honest with himself and knows just how powerful the mating impulse can be in human beings. Call it sex attraction if you want to, but when you've called it that it's important to remember that the mating impulse is the basic, anthropological prime mover. Sex is simply its *modus operandi.*

On Earth and on Mars, whenever a normal man and a normal woman are in close proximity, even for ten or twelve seconds, the mating impulse starts unwinding. On another planet of another star the *modus operandi* may not be sex as we know it, but something quite different, if you can imagine another way of choosing a mate, building a home, and filling it with healthy, happy children.

It's a coiled-spring, trigger-mechanism kind of impulse and neither the man nor the woman have to be attracted to each other on the personality level, unless you want to be technical and regard the purely physical as an attribute of personality. They can be young or old, plain or good looking. Some attraction will be present, even under the most adverse circumstances. But when the woman is young and beautiful and the personality level warm and appealing you'll be deceiving yourself if you think the impulse can be kept from arising just because you already have a mate you're desperately in love with.

You can conquer the impulse if you try hard enough and your love for someone else is strong enough. That's what is meant by loyalty. But you can't keep the impulse from arising and it makes no sense at all to feel guilty about it.

The human brain is a resourceful instrument and there are a dozen ways of keeping a tight grip on your nerves when you wake up on a hospital cot and hear unfamiliar voices talking about you. I chose the way that was most natural to me. I concentrated on the scientific construct I've just summarized, letting my mind glide over, and play around with it for a minute or two and telling myself that I must thank the nurse for all that she had done for me. When Gruff Voice left there would be aglow, a brief moment of warmth between us that might have become a high-leaping flame if I hadn't been in love with Joan and she hadn't been carrying a torch for Gruff Voice.

I wasn't even sure she was beautiful, but it seemed likely, because you can tell a great deal about a woman just from the sound of her voice. Even if she bent over and kissed me, her eyes shining a little because she'd helped me outdistance Death a yard from the finish line and was feeling grateful and thrilled about it...well, that would have been all right too. I didn't think Joan or the man who had just taken her into his arms would have held that kind of kiss against us.

I had the feeling that Gruff Voice was a generous-minded, all right guy, and if an operation had been necessary to save my life he'd done his best to increase my chances with all of the surgical know-how at his command.

Just that thought made me decide to open my eyes and try to raise myself a little, because he had a right to know how grateful I felt.

He was just going through the door. I could see that he was tall, blond and rather sturdily built, but a wave of dizziness made me sink back against the pillows again before I could get a really good look at him. It's hard to tell what a man looks like anyway, when he's facing away from you, and you can only see his disappearing shoulders and the back of his head.

When I opened my eyes for the second time, a full minute later, the eyes that looked back at me were just as I'd pictured them. A deep, lustrous brown. Her face was very much as I'd pictured it too, except that I'd no way of knowing whether she was a blonde or a brunette. She looked a little like Joan. Her hair was done up in a different way, and her lips were a little fuller than Joan's and her cheekbones not quite so prominent. Her nose, too, was a fraction of an inch shorter. But otherwise she could have passed for Joan's sister. Not a twin sister, for the resemblance wasn't anything like that pronounced. But it was close to the family likeness you see quite often in portraits of two sisters when one is smiling and the other looks seriously troubled.

It flashed across my mind that if they had been standing side by side, both wearing the same expression, the resemblance would have been considerably more striking.

It shouldn't have surprised me too much, because of what she'd said to the doctor. Women who think and feel in much the same way are very likely to bear a family resemblance physically. It's the sort of thing that makes an anthropologist shake his head in vigorous denial. But facts are facts and who was I to dispute them?

"Just lie quiet," she whispered, patting me on the shoulder. "Dr. Crawford says you mustn't try to talk. You're going to be all right. I'm Miss Cherubin, your day nurse."

She smiled, her eyes crinkling a little at the corners. "You should have a night nurse too, but I've been staying on in her place."

Cherubin. An angel? No—cherubim was spelt with an "M." And she wasn't *that* young or quite as rosy-cheeked as cherubs are supposed to be.

What made it really tragic was my inability to reach out and touch her or ask her a single question, because right at that moment another wave of dizziness swept over me and I blacked out again.

## CHAPTER ELEVEN

RIGHT AT THIS POINT THERE HAS TO BE a shift in the way I've been recording events as they happened, because what happened next took place elsewhere, while I was flat on my back in the hospital. By "what happened next" I mean...to me and Joan personally and to Commander Littlefield and the Martian Colonization Board and everything

I'd come to Mars to take cognizance of, and do my best to change for the better.

I know, I know. Ten million separate events are taking place all the time on Earth and on Mars and by no stretch of the imagination could they be thought of as an immediate part of this record. But when the threads all start to draw together and tighten about you in a destiny-altering way you have to keep the time-sequence in order and record developments as they take place. Otherwise when they become of immediate concern later on the entire picture will seem out of focus. The frame will start lengthening out and the people in the picture will be out-of-kilter also, and scattered all over the landscape. The only way you can keep them sharply in focus is to record what happens to them *when* it happens.

It shouldn't be too difficult, because there's a seeing eye that hovers over the Mars' Colony day and night. The big Time-Space eye that records everything that takes place in the universe, so that nothing is ever really lost beyond recapture. The past, the present and the future keep flickering, in a backward-forward way, across that immense retina, and some day a technique may be developed for running history off in reverse and you'll see events that took place thousands of years ago as if they were happening today on a lighted screen.

So…let's look through that Big Eye straight down at the Mars Colony, you and I together. And remember. In this particular instance we won't need a history-reversing gimmick at all, because what we'll see and hear is NOW. It starts as a two-person conversation:

"John, I'm frightened. What if the insulation isn't absolutely foolproof? What if one of those Endicott Fuel containers isn't shielded in just the right way? Suppose the radioactive stuff inside builds up to what the nuclear physicists call critical mass and there's an atomic explosion?

Blowups have happened…even in the Endicott Laboratories under the strictest kind of supervision."

"Now look. There's not the slightest danger. Do you think for one moment Endicott would take that big a risk—even though Wendel has the entire combine backed into a corner?"

"They'd take any kind of risk now, because they have no choice. John, if you were going to give me another baby you'd have given me fair warning. I could have steeled myself to endure the harshness and unfairness of it. But when you bring death home with you—"

The woman had been very pretty once. You could see that just by glancing at her. But now her face had a drawn, haggard look and her pallor was more than pronounced. It verged on grayness. Her hair was thinning and turning white and only her eyes remained lustrous, truly alive, as if all that remained of the woman she had once been had been drawn to a focus in the gaze she was training on her husband in desperate appeal.

"Why did you do it, John? You're not just endangering your life and mine. If we didn't have four children…maybe I wouldn't be talking this way."

"I told you I was forced into it, didn't I? Wendel is calling Endicott's bluff. We can no longer go on buying Endicott fuel cylinders openly on margin, hundreds of them and letting all of them stay in Wendel's custody, because we don't really own them at all. The price goes up or the price goes down and we sell out and buy again—and we're supposed to own four-fifths of the Endicott Combine. But there's not a single Colonist who owns the equivalent of four or five cylinders outright. I don't own these six cylinders. But I had to bring them home with me."

"I just don't understand why. It's too complicated for me. A nuclear explosion would be much easier for me to understand."

"All right...I'll go over it again. But try to listen more carefully this time. Before this big, cutthroat war started only one man suspected that one of the two competing combines might try to sell its fluid property to the Colonists on margin. They were supposed to cooperate, not compete, because it was thought that Wendel couldn't possibly keep its nuclear generators operating without fuel. It can't, of course, but only one man suspected that Endicott might refuse to be dwarfed by Wendel in a sharp-practice duel and fight to stay big and powerful by letting the Colonists buy and sell fuel on speculation. That would put the Colonists right in the middle, don't you see?"

"Yes...I do," the woman who had once been almost beautiful said. "Thank you for giving me credit for having that much intelligence. You seem to forget that I have a fairly good memory too. We've gone over this a hundred times."

"Sure we have. But it doesn't seem to have made too deep an impression on you. You can sum it all up by saying that *on paper,* from day to day, it's the Colonists who now own the Endicott Combine, or most of it. So it's the Colonists who are carrying the battle directly to Wendel, fighting for the right to go on wildcatting, to get rich overnight or end up pauperized. It's wildcatting in a sense, just as it was when oil instead of atomic fuel was the big prize to be fought over Earthside. When a Colonist buys Endicott fuel cylinders on margin, it's practically the same as if he were digging an oil well in his own backyard."

"Go on, John," the woman said wearily.

"There's that much uncertainty in it, don't you see? And he's really doing it entirely single-handed and on his own, because he's digging in what is practically a paper graveyard in some respects, unless he's one of the lucky ones. Endicott keeps the fuel. It doesn't go out of their hands. But Wendel still has to buy it directly from the Colonists, who are supposed to own it, and the price fluctuations keep Wendel from becoming all-powerful and Endicott from going under or being dwarfed.

"In the main, it's the Colonists who have most to gain by keeping Endicott powerful and solvent...although the battle lines aren't so tightly drawn that it doesn't become profitable, at times, to go over to the Wendel side. There's a lot of sniping between the lines."

"I know all that, John."

"Well, here's what it all boils down to, what you didn't seem to grasp. You asked me why I brought these six cylinders home. It's because of the one man who did suspect, right from the first, and when the charters were drawn up, that a war of this kind might be waged. I can't even tell you his name. He was probably a minor legal expert or auditor employed by the Board, who had shrewd prophetic gifts...enough foresight, at least...to insert in fine print in both of the charters a provision that Wendel is now using to call Endicott's bluff.

"That provision doesn't say that Endicott can't sell some of their fluid assets on margin. But it sets a limit to that kind of speculative buying and selling. The same limit would apply to Wendel, but Wendel has no fluid assets to sell on margin, and it can't very well break up its generators and big transmission lines and sell them to the Colonists piecemeal, even on margin. It wouldn't look right, because you can't pretend that a fragment of a pipe that is still being operated by a combine is a speculative commodity that has passed into other hands and is subject to day-to-day fluctuations.

"If you want to think of fluid assets as simply a share in a Combine's profits, that's another matter. But I'm not talking about that kind of fluid asset. Endicott has been selling to the Colonists in a literal sense—*moveable fluid assets*. And in fine print in the Endicott charter it says that Endicott can only sell about a third of its fuel cylinders on margin. The others have to be purchased outright and carried home and held by the purchaser until the price is right and he can dispose of them at a profit. Or sell at a loss, as property."

"But you say you didn't buy those cylinders outright. How could you have done that?" the woman protested. "Just one cylinder would cost—a third of a million dollars."

"Naturally I didn't buy them outright. I bought them on margin. But Wendel can't prove that. Endicott is covering up for me and because I've brought them home and can slap my hand on the cool metal and tell Wendel to go to hell if they try to dispute my ownership—Endicott still has a chance to come out on top. Wendel is calling Endicott's bluff, sure. But Endicott is countering with another bluff and they can make it stick. Their auditing department knows just how to do that. So every Colonist who wants to go on wildcatting now has to bring a few cylinders home, to make it look as if he'd bought them outright. Possession puts you nine-tenths on the winning side in any legal argument. You ought to know that!"

"Ought I? Just suppose I did. Would that stop me from becoming terrified, when I know exactly what could happen if the metal isn't as cool as you hope it will be when you slap your hand on it, and the Wendel police stay cold-blooded about it, and wait around for the fissionable material inside to reach critical mass."

"You know damn well it would take an awful lot of accidental jarring and jolting to trigger a fuel cylinder and make it blow up. It probably couldn't happen, *except* in a laboratory where they're careless about such things because of overconfidence."

"Dinner's on the table," the woman said. "We may as well go back into the house while we've still got a home, and gather the children around us, and tell them a few more lies about what the future is going to be like in the Colony, now that one father in three will be bringing nuclear fuel cylinders home with him."

The man—his name was John Lynton—nodded and they returned into the pre-fab. Lynton preceded his wife into the dwelling and the woman paused for an instant in the doorway to stare back at the long metal shed where the six cylinders were reposing...letting her gaze take in as well the double row of foot-high cactus plants which encircled the yard and the sun-reddened stretch of open desert beyond. Then she let the door swing shut behind her, and turned to face her four hungry children.

One thought alone sustained Grace Lynton at that moment. There had never been any need, so far, for the children to go to bed hungry. Their hunger was due solely to the demands of healthy young appetites when dinner was a little delayed and they had been playing strenuously in the yard all afternoon or going on exploring expeditions.

## CHAPTER TWELVE

THEY WERE ALL DOWNSTAIRS NOW, waiting to be fed, hardy perennials like all children everywhere. Thomas with his shining morning face—it seemed to stay that way right up until bedtime—and Susan, seven, and still doll-wedded, and the twins, Hedy and Louise. Three girls and one boy, and Grace Lynton felt a little sorry for her son at times, until she remembered that a boy of thirteen isn't troubled by too many girls in a family when he's seven or eight years their senior. The girls were simply very young children to him and he was—well, right next door at least to being grown up.

"All right," John Lynton said, seating himself at the head of the table. "Let's fall to and see who gets through first."

"Did you have a tough day, Dad?" Thomas asked, reaching for a knife and fork, and drawing a still steaming serving bowl toward him. His unruly hair was so blond it seemed almost white and there was a double row of freckles across the bridge of his nose.

The other three children were brunettes, with hair ranging in color from chestnut brown to jet-black. Even the twins did not closely resemble each other, as non-identical twins so often fail to do.

"Don't annoy your father with questions now, Thomas...please," Grace Lynton said.

"Why not?" Lynton asked, frowning at his wife. "I did have a tough day and there's no sense in soft-pedaling it. Sometimes I almost wish we hadn't come to Mars. No matter how rigorous a Board screening is...there are some things it can't tell you about yourself. Will you make a good father on a world without trees or grass, with no way of getting out into the green countryside and sitting down on the moss-covered bank of a trout stream, with your kid at your side and having a heart to heart talk with him in the cool shade of a big oak or cedar."

"The stew's good, Mom," Thomas said. "Is it all right if I fill up my plate again?"

"Did I ever say you couldn't, Thomas?" Grace Lynton snapped, unable to keep irritation out of her voice, despite her son's compliment. "There'll never be any food shortages in this house, if we have to sell all of the furniture."

"Leave enough for me, Thomas," Hedy Lynton said. "Don't worry, I will," Thomas said. "But if you keep on eating the way you do you'll grow up fat, and no man in the

Colony will marry a fat woman when there are so many thin ones."

"That's very well put, Thomas," Lynton said. "I have a brilliant son—practically a genius. But don't let it go to your head, boy. Unless you're in the electronic field or have some other technical specialty a straightforward, rugged he-man can do more for the Colony."

"What kind of talk is that, John?" Grace Lynton demanded. "There's nothing unmanly about a genius, in any field."

"No, I suppose not. But I wouldn't want him to be a poet or a painter. They just stand back and observe life and I'd like to see my son wade in fighting."

The daylight outside had started fading before Lynton and his wife had returned indoors. But now the quickly-arriving Mars' night was almost at hand, and the twilight had deepened outside and was giving way to complete darkness at the edge of the desert.

The two adults and four children seated about the table hadn't once glanced toward the window, for the food and contentious conversation had absorbed all of their attention.

It was Thomas who saw the light first, flickering on and off close to the shed. He had always wanted, deep down, in a secret way that he had never dared to discuss with anyone, to be an artist and paint at least a hundred pictures that would show the people who looked at them exactly what life on Mars was like. And his father's gaze, trained upon him in such a steady way, had made him squirm inwardly, as if his secret might at any moment be exposed. To avoid his father's gaze he'd looked straight out the window and seen the strange light flickering on and off.

"Dad!" he said.

"What is it, son?"

"There's a light moving around out in the yard, close to the shed."

If Thomas had suddenly toppled over dead his father could not have leapt up from the table with more horror in his eyes.

"Why...why...Good God! Wendel wouldn't go *that* far! It would be an act of madness!"

"John, you don't think—"

Thomas' mother was on her feet too now, her face drained of all color, her eyes darting to the window and back to the tight-lipped, violently trembling man at the head of the table. John Lynton's face had gone as white as her own.

For a minute Thomas thought that his father was going to rush right out into the yard and grab hold of the intruder, as fast as he'd leapt up from the table. Then he saw he'd guessed wrong about that.

Lynton crossed the room in five long strides, swung open the weapon locker and grabbed hold of a holstered handgun instead. He strapped the holster to his waist before whipping out the weapon and snapping off the safety mechanism.

He was starting for the door when Grace Lynton called out warningly: "John, don't! *John!*"

He swung about, staring at her in consternation. "Don't what? If they've tampered with those cylinders I'll make sure they won't live to blow up another man's home—or half the Colony!"

"You can't blast them down!" Her voice rose shrilly. "No, John! A handgun blast that close to a fuel cylinder would set off a chain reaction—"

"No, it won't. The blast is channeled. Don't be a fool, Grace. I know what I'm doing."

"You're the fool! You'll get us all killed!"

"If they've tampered with just one of those cylinders we won't have to worry about what a handgun blast will do. But they won't save their own skins before the *big* blast hits us. That's one thing I can make sure of."

He turned and was gone. She started to follow him out into the yard, but became aware of how dangerous that would be just in time. If she followed her husband the children would almost certainly follow her, for she couldn't order them to stay indoors and hope to be obeyed.

She rushed to the window and stared out, her face pressed to the pane.

She could feel Thomas pressing close to her—or was it Hedy or Susan? There was a heaviness in his body, which made her almost sure it was Thomas. But that meant nothing, because she loved all of her children equally.

Suddenly she was sure it was Thomas, because he was speaking to her. "Take it easy, Mom! Dad'll take care of whoever it is. He's got a handgun to protect him."

"Oh, I know he has!" she wanted to scream. "It will be a beautiful way of protecting us all...by sending us straight into eternity. God, dear God, don't let him blast. Don't—" The blast came then, lighting up the darkness outside, making the windowpanes rattle. For an instant Grace Lynton could see her husband clearly, standing by the shed with a white flare spreading outward from his shoulders.

Then the flare dwindled and vanished and Grace Lynton had no way of knowing what had happened outside in the dark. She was sure of only one thing. She couldn't stay inside the house with her husband moving about a few feet from fuel cylinders that might blow up at any moment, for there was at least a fifty percent likelihood that the intruder had accomplished what he'd come to do, before Thomas had seen the light bobbing about in the yard.

She had straightened and was hugging her son to her, just starting to turn, when John Lynton's voice rang out sharply from the doorway.

"Grace! I blasted at him but he got away! Listen carefully. I've only a moment to talk."

He was standing in the doorway with the handgun reholstered at his waist, its handle gleaming dully. His pallor was startling, for it went far beyond mere paleness, as if all the blood had been drawn from his face artificially, leaving the skin gray and shrunken.

"I can't be sure, but I think...one of the cylinders has been triggered to blow up," he went on quickly. "It isn't heating up. There'd be no heat—just a faint vibration. When I put my hand on the metal I was almost sure I could feel a vibration. We've got just one chance of staying alive—and I'll have to move fast. I'm going to take it to the Spaceport— I can get there in the conveyor truck in ten minutes—and have them dismantle it. They'll know how. I don't. I'll take all six of the cylinders, to make sure."

"John, no! It will blow up in the truck. I'm sure of it. We'd better all get out in the desert, as far away from it as we can. If we start right now and run—"

"We could go in the truck, Dad!" Thomas cried.

Lynton shook his head. "If just one cylinder blows up—it will take three miles of desert with it. If all six go...twenty miles of desert. There are at least six thousand Colonists within three or four miles of us. There are less than a thousand people at the Spaceport. Only one big sky ship is still unloading. Better a thousand deaths than six or seven thousand...if it blows up before they can dismantle it."

"But John— Oh, God, I don't know."

"It's the best way, the surest way. We can't think only of ourselves. If I drove straight out into the desert with it and it blows up within twenty minutes the fallout would still kill several thousand Colonists. The Spaceport's in the other direction, completely isolated. And I can get there in fifteen minutes…even if I'm stopped by the Wendel police and have to blast my way to it."

"Why should they try to stop you? They'd die themselves—"

"Why did they send someone to trigger that bomb? They'll take any risk now, because they know that Endicott's new bluff could smash them. That cylinder is smaller than the first atomic bomb ever built—much smaller than the one that was dropped on Hiroshima—and if they have to explode a half-dozen of them in different parts of the Colony to demoralize the Colonists and discredit Endicott they're prepared to do it, apparently. Even if it kills thirty thousand people. Or maybe they figured the one I'm taking to the Spaceport—and I *am* taking it there, Grace—would make the Colonists think twice about taking any more Endicott fuel cylinders home with them."

"You're right, John," Grace Lynton said, with a firmness in her voice which surprised her. "We can't think only of ourselves. Until you come back—every moment will be a living death. But—you must do it. There's no other way."

"I'll be back," Lynton said. "I—I love you, Grace."

"And I love you, John—even though I've said cruel, cutting things at times. I love you very much."

"Take care of yourself, Dad," Thomas said.

"I will, son. Don't worry. Just be the man of the family and keep the kids in line until I get back."


## CHAPTER THIRTEEN

I HAD NO WAY OF KNOWING HOW LONG I remained on the outer fringes of what was probably just a weakness-produced blackout before the outlines of the hospital room wavered back, becoming so clear again that I could see the foot of the bed, and a glass-topped table covered with small bottles and a roll of gauze bandage that looked about as big as a liquid fuel cylinder.

Someone who couldn't have been the doctor was sitting in a chair by the bed, leaning a little forward, his eyes level with mine. I was more than startled. An ice-cold measuring worm came out at the base of my spine and started inching its way upward, bunching itself up and lengthening out again, the way measuring worms do when they're trying to decide if you're just the right fit for a human-style coffin.

I had a visitor whose face would have chilled a perfectly well man prepared to defend himself against violence at the drop of a hat. He was looking at me with a glacial animosity in his stare, as if he resented the fact that I was still alive and would do something about it if I gave him the slightest encouragement.

Even without encouragement I had the feeling that my life hung by a thread which could snap at any moment, so long as he remained that close to me with no one standing by to interfere if he lost control of himself.

He didn't have a moronic or particularly brutal looking face. Intelligence of a high order had given his features a cast you couldn't mistake. It was the kind of look that went with disciplined thinking—long years of it—and behavior that was based on intellectual discernment, however much that discernment had been abused during moments of uncontrollable rage. Uncontrollable rage, as every psychologist knows, can tie the reasoning part of any man's mind into knots. Everything that was primitive in him seemed to be at the helm now, as if he bore me so much ill-will that he might be capable of trying to take my life with just his bare hands, if he happened to be unarmed. And I was far from sure of that.

His glacial gray eyes seemed to say: "I've got you exactly where I want you, chum. It won't do you any good to shout for help. It stands to reason that if I could get in here to talk to you at a time like this, throwing my weight around a little further would be no problem at all. Five minutes of privacy will suit me fine. After all, how long will killing you take?"

He was a fairly big man, compactly built, with hands that looked strong enough to bend a steel bar, if he didn't mind chancing a rush of blood to the head that might have been a little risky in a man his age.

I had no idea why he was sitting there, only that the alarm bells were ringing again. Only this time it wasn't taking place in a crowded subway train in total darkness, or up near the top of a swaying spiral where an assassin's aim could be a little less than sure. It was man to man, tete-a-tete, in a well-lighted hospital room.

I was flat on my back and weak as hell and Death was looking straight at me out of ice-blue eyes. I had only one straw to clutch at. The hospital room might just possibly be under surveillance and an act of violence that's likely to boomerang can give an assassin pause.

His first words ripped that straw from me and crumpled it up, with such vigor I was sure I could hear a crunching sound.

"I've just a few questions to ask you," he said, in a surprisingly mild tone. "We've made sure that there are no recording devices in this room. We always make a careful check as a matter of routine, when we're forced to demand complete privacy during an interrogation of this sort. It's something we'd prefer not to do, but there are times—"

He shrugged, as if he'd made the point clear enough and resented the necessity of making it any plainer.

117

"When the internal security of the Colony is endangered," he went on impatiently, "we do not hesitate to invoke all of our authority. We have no choice. Too many people take it for granted that a privately owned combine is exceeding its authority when it undertakes police investigations not specifically authorized by its charter. They forget that such police powers are implicit in every charter, which provides for the exercise of reasonable vigilance in the public domain. Safeguarding the public, which Wendel Atomics serves, would not be possible if we did not exercise such authority."

How true that was I didn't have enough legal knowledge at my fingertips to decide. But I was pretty sure it was a bald-faced lie. But just his use of the word "power" explained how he'd managed to get as close to me as he'd done, with no one within earshot to hear me if I burst my lungs shouting.

The kind of power the Board had given me the right to exercise superseded whatever display of authority Wendel Atomics had used to turn the hospital room into a prison cell. But who would know or make a move to save me—if the silver bird didn't get a chance to flap its wings on my uniform until they were pumping embalming fluid into my veins and making plans to lower me, with a ceremonial flourish, into a desert grave?

"There are a few things Wendel Atomics has a right to know," Glacial Stare was saying. "A legal right—make no mistake about that. I'd advise you not to lie to me. If you do—"

He shrugged again.

I said something then that surprised me, because I didn't think right at the moment I had that much defiance on tap.

"Shove it!" I said.

He couldn't have heard me, because he went on with no change of expression. "Commander Littlefield is within his rights in refusing to permit us to question him as to what took place on board the Mars' rocket. We have no jurisdiction over such…irregularities in space. If we questioned just one of his officers, the Board would have every right to revoke our charter. But two of the officers have come to us and voluntarily submitted information, which we cannot ignore. We believe that the internal security of the Colony is in danger and we intend to take steps to make sure that none of the questions we have a right to ask will remain unanswered."

He was laying it on the line, all right, speaking with an almost surgical kind of precision, so that I couldn't claim later—if I turned stubborn—that I'd failed to understand him. It's funny how a man who's holding all the cards will sometimes do that, just on the off-chance that you may have an ace up your sleeve and may use it to make trouble for him later on.

He must have been pretty sure I didn't have a concealed ace, however, for he backed up what he was saying with the most dangerous kind of threat. Dangerous to him…if there *had* been a hidden listening device in the room and a tape with that threat on it had come to the attention of the Board.

"I hope, for your sake," he said, "that you'll keep nothing back. It is very unpleasant to sit in a Big-Image interrogation room and have part of your mind destroyed. The part you value most that makes you what you are—destroyed, sliced away. Yes…*sliced away* is quite accurate, even though no instrument would be needed and not a hand would be laid on you. You can cut deep into the brain with vibrations alone. But nothing…*physical* ever takes place in the Big-Image interrogation room. No knife or vibrator, as you know. The destruction is brought about in a quite different way. But it's just as drastic and irreversible as a prefrontal lobotomy."

He stopped talking abruptly, looking past me at the opposite wall, as if he could already see the shadow of a broken and tormented man projected there. I could see it too, and I didn't like to think that I was coming that close to sharing his thoughts. But it was useless to pretend that the man who was casting that shadow might not turn out to be me.

So they had them on Mars, too, with the Wendel police on hand to make sure that the big screen with its multiple sound tracks and the smoothly operating projector were kept carefully hidden from the law. Big-Image interrogation rooms—a cruel vestige of the brainwashing techniques that had so outraged world opinion in the middle decades of the twentieth century that they had been castigated and outlawed by the United Nations, the World Court and every responsible Governmental agency on Earth.

But the criminal mind has very little respect for world opinion or restrictions on brutal practices that are very difficult to enforce. Big-Image interrogation had begun as a police investigation procedure, which made it easy for the wrong kind of police force to resort to it and claim historic precedent and moral justification as a cover-up if their activities ever came to light.

I was sure that Glacial Stare had mentioned it solely to turn the screw as far as it would go, hoping I'd turn pale and answer his questions in a completely cooperative way. I was sure that if I did he'd stop threatening me immediately, listen with attentive ear to what I had to say and apologize for letting me think, even for a moment, that it was just a part of my mind he'd been planning to destroy. Why should he want to upset me that way, when the only thing he'd had in mind from the start was to persuade me to talk and then relieve me of all anxiety by killing me?

He wasn't giving me credit for having the kind of brain it would have been worth taking the trouble to destroy, even in part, but there was nothing to be gained by reminding him of that.

You don't have to be a professional historian or even a data-collecting research specialist in the police procedure field to pinpoint the origin of Big-Image interrogation in the middle years of the twentieth century.

Three out of five well-informed people can tell you exactly how it began, if you jog them into remembering by showing them a micro-film recording of what took place during just one of those interrogations sixty or seventy years ago.

My memory didn't need to be jogged. I'd examined too many micro-film recordings made even earlier than that—so many years before I was born that the grooves have to be altered if you want to run them off in the projectors that were in common use at the turn of the century, because they ante-date even those old-style machines.

As early as 1965 someone had discovered and pointed out that the cinema was no longer just an entertainment medium. Everyone at the time, I suppose, had made that discovery already, in a private sort of way, but an entire society can have a blind spot and go right on clinging to established patterns of thought, if only because people in general are a little reluctant to discuss openly anything that threatens to overturn the apple cart.

At any rate, about 1965 someone whose name has not come down to us—quite possibly he was a drama critic, that most curious of breeds—had pointed out that the cinema had become a potentially mind-shattering instrument of torture, which could be used to brainwash a spectator until he became a hopeless psychotic, incapable of distinguishing reality from illusion. Schizophrenic or manic depressive, take your pick.

It was the bigger-than-life illusion that could do that—the strange, often terrifying sense of being caught up in some super-reality that had no real existence in time or space, in the ordinary way that time-and-space manifests itself to us in everyday life.

The cinema became potentially that kind of torture medium the instant the first of the twenty-million-dollar spectacles in full color appeared on the screen.

We know what that kind of illusion can do today and when we watch a screen spectacle that distorts reality for three or four hours by making everything seem fifty or a hundred times as large as life...we make sure that we are entering a theater that is Government supervised and not a Big-Image interrogation room presided over by a sadist in police uniform.

Everyone knows how it is today, and stays on guard, perpetually alert. But back in the twentieth century the danger wasn't clearly understood, and that lack of understanding was taken advantage of by the brainwashers in uniform to exact confessions at a terrible price.

Everyone is familiar with the disorientation I'm talking about. Even the old stage plays and the earlier black-and-white movies and not a few books could bring it about to some extent, when you left the theater or closed the book, and passed from a world of dramatically heightened illusion into the drabness of everyday life.

But the big screen spectacles in full color, with electronic sound effects, make the world of illusion and the world of sober reality seem as far apart as two contradictory constructs in symbolic logic. When you look at that kind of motion picture you get the illusion that all of the events on the screen, even the intimate, two-person close-ups, are taking place on a gigantic scale.

The sharpness and brightness of everything, the brilliance of the colorama, the dramatic selectivity which makes each scene burn its way into your brain as a titan encounter in a world of giants is so overwhelming that when you emerge from the theater after watching such a film the world of reality seems small, stunted, anemic by contrast.

You look at the men and women walking past you on the street and they seem to have nothing in common with the men and women you've just seen on the screen. That quiet little guy puffing on a cigarette and returning your stunned stare with a perplexed frown may be the director of a big power combine, with just as much lightning at his fingertips. But he seems like a pygmy. It would be impossible to visualize him as a helmeted giant stripped to the waist, breasting wild seas at the helm of a Viking ship or a space-suited giant in a colorama with a present-day background.

In the big screen spectacles all of the men seem gigantic, with tremendous, muscular torsos. Even the little guys look like titan figures, fifty or a hundred times as large as they seem outside the theater. And the women—with the possible exception of the very feminine ones with overwhelming sex appeal—look like Amazons.

You can't even equate the violence you encounter in everyday life with the violence that takes place in a big screen spectacle. After you've watched the spectacle kind of violence for three or four hours an army equipped with the most formidable of modern weapons, closing in on a half bombed out city would look infinitely less formidable—toy soldiers in a kindergarten world which the big-image, colorama giants could topple and scatter just by inflating their cheeks and blowing on them.

Even the Big Mushroom, which we've miraculously managed to keep from blowing Earth apart for almost a century now, looks fifty times as destructive when you see it on the screen, spiraling skyward as the crowning spectacle of a sound-color, fifty-million-dollar Armageddon.

But remember this. It doesn't cost anything like that much to put four or five giants from that kind of motion picture on a screen in a Big-Image interrogation room. The cost, in fact, is negligible, because just one scene can be repeated over and over. You're seated all alone in the middle of what looks like a medieval torture chamber—if you leave out the racks and thumbscrews and iron maidens and just think of such a chamber as a blank-walled, cell-like horror— and on the screen, fifty or a hundred times life-size, are the lads who have been given the task of cutting you down to size.

*You're* still very much a part of the puny world outside the theater you've lived in most of your life. You know it, you feel it...you can't escape from it. When a big screen production has been designed solely to entertain you, you can identify yourself with the giants to some extent. You become a part of the illusion. But how can you identify with four or five brutish looking lads with no resemblance to yourself, with a look on their faces which says they hate your guts and are out for blood and won't be satisfied until they've brain-washed you.

Oh, it looks easy. Resistance, laughing in their faces, should be no problem at all, because you know damn well it's nothing but an illusion.

But just how long do you think you can go on believing that those Neanderthaler types with five-pronged metal whiplashes dangling from their wrists aren't flesh-and-blood tormentors?

All right, you still think it should be easy. All I can say is...just sit for five hours in a Big-Image interrogation room and try staying sane. Go ahead, insist on being granted that privilege. It might be a little difficult to come as close to it as I was right at that moment, flat on my back in a hospital bed with Glacial Stare reminding me just how terrible it could be. But you never know until you try. On Mars bringing that about shouldn't be too difficult...with Wendel Atomics determined to build up a reputation for ruthlessness to protect its interests in the war it was waging with Endicott Fuel and all of the colonists who were being forced to wildcat in a commodity field so explosive that it could turn them into killers of the dream and blow them apart for good measure.

But let's go back to the Big-Image interrogation room for a moment. You're sitting there, staring up at the Neanderthaler-type giants and they're staring down at you. Their eyes are slitted and they're stripped to the waist and there is a fine sheen of sweat on their chests. There is nothing trim or athletic looking about them. They're heavyset, almost muscle-bound, with the outsize, very ugly-looking kind of physical massiveness you see in some wrestlers, but hardly ever in a professional boxer even in the heavyweight class.

"Well, pal!" one of them says, winking at you.

"I have an idea he'd like to high-hat us," another chimes in, winking also, but at Muscle Bound Number One instead of at you.

"We'll have to do something about that," Muscle Bound Number Three insists.

"Oh, we will...we will. But we ought to give him a little time to get better acquainted with us. Maybe we can soften him up a little just by talking to him. What do you say?"

"Sure, why not? You see a guy flat on his face, with his skull bashed in, and you start feeling sorry for him. Right off, that's bad. It keeps you from really setting to work on him."

At first you can laugh, almost, because who ever heard of a screen giant stepping out from the screen and slashing you across the chest with a five-pronged metal whiplash? But if you know what's coming you don't feel much like laughing, even at first.

Because...it goes on and on and on. It builds up and there's no way you can shut it out, because they inject a drug just under your eyelids which forces you to keep your eyes open. You can't close them no matter how hard you try. And you can't turn your head aside, because you're strapped to the seat and there's a clamp at the back of your head that prevents you from moving it.

It goes on and on, and after a while the giants are no longer on the screen, but right in the interrogation room with you. One of them is raising and lowering his arm, bringing the whiplash down on your bare shoulders... You can feel the thongs cutting into your flesh, and not even screaming will put a stop to it, because you can't put a stop to an illusion that is ripping your mind apart and letting all of the sanity drain out of you.

It's the hundred-times-bigger-than-life gimmick that does it, although that slang-neat little word doesn't begin to do justice to what a Big-Image interrogation can do to you. They're big, *big,* BIG, with all the brutishness blown up, and showing on their faces. And they seem to be leaning out from the screen before they emerge from it and you can hear the whiplash swishing through the air and the sound of it is magnified too, and just the whiplash alone seems large enough to rip the hide off a mastodon.

Worst of all, that hundred-times-bigger-than-life illusion doesn't depend on size alone, as I've pointed out. It depends on the over-all magnification of reality that takes place in a big screen spectacle, the disorientation that makes the real world seem to shrivel into insignificance.

It seldom takes longer than five hours to complete the brainwashing. You pass through three stages. At the end of an hour—or two, at most—when the torment becomes almost unbearable you start to hallucinate a little, but you're still sane enough to answer most of the questions they ask you. Then you become so hopelessly psychotic that your answers can no longer be relied on. But they're satisfied, they've got what they wanted from you when they started the interrogation.

Without wasting any more time they go on to the third stage. They calm you down and "cure" you with the mental torture equivalent of a prefrontal lobotomy. They do that to make sure you'll lose the part of your mind that can resent what's been done to you, and summon enough will power to turn accuser.

And now I was lying flat on my back, unsure of how much strength was left in me, and Glacial Stare was threatening me with *that!* Not just an hour or two with the barrel-chested lads—on rare occasions they stopped just short of the third stage—but the full, deep-cut treatment.


## CHAPTER FOURTEEN

HE'D MADE IT PLAIN THAT HE WAS representing Wendel. But he hadn't come right out and identified himself, and I had no way of knowing exactly what kind of Wendel agent he was. The worst kind, beyond a doubt. But what I would have liked to know took in more territory than that.

Was he…a replacement? Had he been instructed to step into the shoes of the secret agent the robot had killed in space? If he had, the satisfaction he'd get from killing me would probably exceed the pleasure a run-of-the-mill Wendel police officer would experience.

It would be easier for him to identify with the slain crewman and feel a sense of personal outrage strong enough to make him think of himself as an avenger. The fact that he wasn't wearing a uniform lent support to that grim possibility. When a man has a strong personal reason for wanting you dead it can make the official reason seem twice as urgent. It could also bring into his face the kind of look that Glacial Stare was still keeping trained on me.

There was only one thing I knew with absolute certainty. Answering his questions would do me no good—would only make the danger greater the instant I stopped talking. I'd be signing my own death warrant with a vengeance if I co-operated with him right there in the hospital room and spared him the trouble of having me bound and gagged and smuggled out of the hospital into a Big-Image interrogation room.

Why make him a present of the only card I was holding? Why be that charitable when… God, how silly could you get? If I'd had my strength or there had been anyone within earshot to dispute his authority if I shouted for help—a one in fifty-chance of it, even—I might have been holding at least a Jack or a Queen. But never an Ace, or four of a kind or a Royal Flush. About all I was holding was the joker. In some games the joker can be the highest card in the deck, but not in the kind of game the three of us were playing.

It was the third player who was holding all of the really high cards. He was hovering just behind Glacial Stare, with a shroud with my name embroidered on it draped over his arm. He could see my hand clearly, because he was looking straight at me out of eyes like holes in a skull.

That scythe-and-sickle round is almost unbeatable because of the way Death has of just quietly raising the ante until all hope is gone. Sometimes you've no choice but to let him call your bluff, lay your cards face up on the table, and wait for the blow to fall.

Sometimes…but not always. Death is a weird-o who doesn't really want anyone to live to a crusty old age and that can anger you, and there are no limits to what a certain kind of resentment can do for you. You'll take desperate chances when you know the sands have just about run out.

I came up out of the bed so fast the electricity my body generated made the sheets crackle. It wasn't the helplessly weak body I'd thought it. Not at all. When I whipped back my arm I could feel a thrust of power and resilience in my shoulder muscles that amazed me, because it shouldn't have been there. There was no flabbiness or lack of muscle tone.

I crashed into him before my feet hit the floor, sinking my fist into his mid-section and sending the chair he was sitting in skidding half across the hospital room.

He clung to both arms of the chair, too jolted to straighten up and try to heave himself out of it before I shortened the distance between us by hurling myself directly at him again. I just missed fumbling that crucial follow-up, because my legs were deficient in muscle tone and they almost collapsed under me before I got to him.

I dragged him out of the chair and had him down on the floor and was banging his head against the floor before he could get any kind of grip on me. I wasn't in the least bit gentle about it. If I'd been banging him around for five or ten minutes without stopping I couldn't have heightened the look of shock and absolute horror in his eyes.

The best he could do was twist about under me and try desperately to raise himself a little, thrusting his head forward to keep me from bringing it so violently into contact with the floor. He seemed to be trying so hard to get out, from under that I decided to help him. I lifted him clean off the floor and slammed him back against the wall—not once, but several times.

I don't know where my strength came from, but even my legs were doing all right now. They were still the weakest part of me, but they went right on supporting me until I finished clouting him with something that was just as good as a sledgehammer—the firm wall itself, completely stationary as it was. If I'd been standing behind it using it as a forward-thrusting shield his skull couldn't have cracked against it any harder.

I suppose it wasn't really the hospital room wall I was clouting him with, because, as I say, it was stationary. But when you're extracting the fangs of a dangerous little reptile who has just threatened you with Big-Image interrogation and know that your strength may give out at any moment cause and effect get swallowed up in an urgency that can distort reality. His face was a confused blur for a moment. But a second or two before all of the expression drained out of it and he slumped jerkily to the floor my vision steadied and I saw that his look of absolute horror had been replaced by the deadliest kind of hatred.

It's always a little jolting, no matter how you slice it, to know that a man who should be incapable of feeling anything but shock and pain can pass out cold with that kind of look in his eyes.

I'd gone berserk for a moment, but when I have to, when there's some compelling reason for it, I can cool off fast. *Calm down* would be a more accurate way of phrasing it, for I knew it would take a long time for the way I felt about Glacial Stare to turn from anger to enlightened scientific detachment. He couldn't really help being what he was, because what is known as the bastard-pattern gets grooved into the poor unhappy devils that are afflicted with it way back in childhood. They injure themselves more than they injure others, even though what they do to others in the process often doesn't bear thinking about.

Right at the moment Glacial Stare had injured himself, but not deliberately. I had done most of the injuring for him. But there would be times when he'd punish himself twice as remorselessly, and he'd go on doing it to the end of his days. If there's a hell on Earth the sadistic bastards occupy it, and it's unscientific to feel anything but pity for them.

It was equally unscientific for me to feel anything but concern for my own safety right at the moment, because I was still trapped in a hospital room with all of the physical weakness I'd felt a few minutes before creeping back and with no guarantee that if I walked out of the room in a tottering condition I wouldn't run smack into another Wendel agent.

Quite possibly they had the hospital surrounded and when they saw what I'd done to Glacial Stare they wouldn't talk with me as long as he had done before I'd belted him unconscious.

They'd either blast me down, cold-bloodedly and on the spot, with one of the compact little handguns Doctor Mile-Away had discussed with Joan on the ambulance—how many days, weeks away that ride seemed—or gag and bind me and carry me out on a stretcher.

Glacial Stare himself no longer worried me. He'd be out for as long as it would take me to decide whether it would be better to go staggering out of the hospital room and trust the first person I collided with not to betray me, or flop back on the bed and shout for help from there.

You do crazy things, sometimes, when you're that uncertain. There wasn't a chance of his coming to immediately, but just automatically I crouched beside him and rolled one of his eyelids back with my thumb. The glazed pupil that stared sightlessly back at me gave me a jolt, because it could have meant that I'd killed him. I thrust my hand under his shirt and felt around for a heartbeat and found no trace of one. His skin was clammy and very cold.

Then I saw that he was still breathing. His chest rose and fell and there was a sudden, dull thumping where my palm was resting.

All right, that took care of him. He would live to turn vicious again. But it didn't take care of me. I was still in the worst kind of danger, and sounding off might be the unwisest thing I could do. But what chance would I have otherwise? Someone would have to know or I'd likely as not take all of the wrong risks.

I had to fight off the weakness that was coming back and be ready for anything—even a set-to with another Wendel agent or a half-dozen of them. But I had to have an ally, someone who knew the hospital as well as I knew the lines: of my palm. I had to be briefed in advance, or I'd have no way of knowing how good my chances were.

How long could I stay on my feet, despite the weakness, if I decided on a desperate gamble and attempted to get out of the hospital alive? Did any of the doctors have enough authority to oppose Wendel, if I told them who I was and they believed me. Or did Wendel have so much power here they'd have to actually see the silver bird to take risks on my behalf which would bring the entire staff an exceptional courage citation from the Board—if I lived to set the record straight.

And where was the silver bird and my secret-code identification papers? Not on my person. All of my clothes had been removed and I was wearing just a one-piece, in-patient garment with no pockets in it. It stood to reason they'd gone through my clothes before attaching a tag to them and ruing them away, on the off chance I might live to reclaim them. In an emergency case they'd have displayed that much curiosity, at least. It would have been no more than a routine procedure.

Unless—Commander Littlefield had warned them not to tamper with my clothes and to return them to him immediately. No, no—that was crazy. The chances were he'd removed the silver bird and the identification papers from my inner breast pocket before they'd bundled me into the ambulance and they were now safely in his possession.

Or perhaps Joan had them. It was all pure guesswork, but I was fairly certain of one thing. They hadn't found the silver bird or Glacial Stare would never have been permitted—

Hell…why not face it. I couldn't even be completely sure of that. If Wendel was all-powerful here the doctors' hands would be tied, no matter how much they knew about me. I'd have to be in robust health and on my feet, with the silver bird gleaming on my shoulder, to overcome that kind of power.

Actually, I didn't think Commander Littlefield had told them anything. It was the kind of secret he'd guard with his life, unless he'd had reason to suspect that Wendel would send an agent to kill me before I had a chance to tell him whether or not I thought the danger was great enough to justify abandoning all secrecy…immediately and as a simple safety precaution. He'd respect my wishes in the matter, and could certainly be excused for not having had the foresight to take maximum precautions on his own initiative. It could very easily be argued that he should have done so…that he had blundered badly. But I refused to condemn him for keeping the secrecy obligation so firmly in mind that he'd failed to realize precisely how fast and ruthlessly Wendel could move. And even if I'd been ringed about with security precautions Wendel might have succeeded in convincing the hospital staff that the silver bird was a lead counterfeit and Littlefield an anti-Colony conspirator.

A lot of suspicion hovered over the heads of the big sky ship commanders, anyway—a sinister, shadowy aura woven of lies and slander that accompanied them everywhere and greatly curtailed their authority when they attempted to intervene in the affairs of the Colony.

All that passed through my mind as I stood staring down at Glacial Stare and helped me come to a decision. If I lived to get out of the hospital I'd be on my own with a vengeance.

But Littlefield was still my best bet. I'd be completely alone in totally unfamiliar surroundings, facing a challenge such as no man had ever faced before and survived to tell about it.

I'd have to make my way through the Colony on foot, a stranger in a world I'd had no time to adjust to and get back to the sky ship somehow—even if it meant talking my way into the good graces of criminals and hiding in dark alleys and learning new ways of thinking and acting the hard way—but fast—and resorting to every dodge in the book to keep one jump ahead of the Wendel agents.

There'd be a hue and cry—and they'd be out for my blood. I had no identification papers—nothing. I'd be as naked and vulnerable as the day I was born in more ways than one—except that I'd be a grown man in body and mind with a grown man's resourcefulness.

I could only hope I'd prove equal to the task and acquit myself well and succeed in silencing the skeptical part of myself that was shaking its head in furious disbelief.

I'd decided to make no attempt to get anyone into the room by sounding off. Much as I needed an ally, the risk would be too great. No one had come rushing in, and the fact that I'd been able to prevent Glacial Stare from uttering a sound by taking him by complete surprise and battering his skull against the wall until he folded was a point in my favor. Not to regard it as a break and take full advantage of it would have been foolish.

Slipping quickly from the room and taking my chances made more sense than waiting around for an ally to come to my assistance, because he might not be an ally at all, but another Wendel agent.

I was deliberately shutting my mind to the greatest danger—the Big One.

You're deliberately shutting your mind to the Big One, Ralphie boy. Getting back to the sky ship will be tough sledding, every foot of the way, and you'll have to dodge and weave about and you may end up dead in the darkest of Martian alleys, half blown apart by an atomic handgun. But the Big One is getting out of the hospital itself, and you're afraid to let yourself think about that because you know how heavily the odds will be stacked against you.

You don't know what the hospital is like—how big it is, even. You don't know how many corridors there are, or how many alarm bells will start ringing the instant anyone sees you. There may be a dozen nurses to a floor and doctors constantly on the move from the operating rooms to the recovery wards, and a Wendel agent or two on guard at the end of each corridor.

All the exits may be blocked, with Wendel agents armed with atomic handguns just waiting for you to show up running. You don't even know how far the hospital is from the center of the Colony, only that—just before you blacked out for the last time in the ambulance—you seemed to be quite a distance from the heart of the Colony.

Even if there are no guards at any of the exits and no one tries to stop you how will you be able to find your way back to the spaceport without a compass if the hospital is ten or fifteen miles from the Colony, and all about you is a waste of desert sand and there are no outgoing ambulances standing by to give you a lift.

High up in one of the rooms there'll be a Wendel agent you've belted into insensibility and he'll be stirring and calling out for help and when they come swarming into the hospital room to lift him up—the nurses and the doctors who can't help but blanch a little when he reminds them just how powerful the Wendel Combine is—he'll have only one thing to say to them.

"Get me the Central Police Agency on the telecommunicator."

You'll be out in the red desert, fighting your way toward the Colony through a sandstorm perhaps, but ten or twelve minutes after that call goes through you'll hear a droning overhead and that will be the end of you.

The hell of it was—no man ever needed an ally more desperately. I needed a confederate, right at that moment in the room with me, if only because I couldn't hope to cheat death for ten minutes running if I ever reached the streets of the Colony without some Colony-type clothes to replace the one-piece, in-patient garment I was wearing. A doctor's white smock wouldn't do, and neither would a nurse's uniform. I didn't have the right build to pass for a nurse even inside the walls of the hospital, not to mention the craggy cast of my features and the heavy growth of stubble which covered my cheeks.

## CHAPTER FIFTEEN

FAR BACK IN THE TWENTIETH CENTURY, when World War II was just coming to a close, the anti-Nazi underground movement had helped quite a few soldiers escape from prison camps disguised as women. It certainly wasn't a stratagem to be rejected out of hand, when your life was at stake. But somehow my masculine pride was affronted by the thought and I did not take kindly to it.

There had to be a lot of male patient's clothes hanging somewhere in the hospital, but how was I to get my hands on a complete outfit if I had to leave the hospital like a thief in the night, just one leap ahead of Death in a Wendel police uniform?

Stealth? Would that solve it? If I moved very cautiously at first, putting the thought of what could happen out of my mind, and trying to find a room where clothes were hanging?

No—I couldn't afford to move too cautiously. I'd have to move fast and boldly, trusting to blind luck to protect me. But the clothes problem still remained, and unless I could solve it—

She solved it for me. I didn't know that at first and neither did she—I mean, she had no idea when she came back into the room that any such problem would confront her. All she saw was Glacial Stare lying slumped against the wall, his jaw sagging and the patient she'd left flat on his back a short while before standing in the middle of the room with his in-patient garment twisted grotesquely about his bony, knobby knees and looking one hell of a mess. It's always been hard for me to understand how a woman can find the angular, bony body of a man attractive, especially when it's in a state of half-undress. But there's no explaining the mystery of sex, and I'll give her this much—she didn't give me a second glance for a moment. She had eyes only for Glacial Stare. She stood staring down at him with all the blood draining from her face, as if she'd never seen a dead man before or a man as close to death as Glacial Stare seemed to be.

I saw the scream coming just in time, I stepped in front of her and clamped my hand over her mouth, drawing her close to me, and keeping a tight grip on her shoulder to prevent her from breaking away from me and making a dash for the door.

I couldn't blame her for being scared or feeling, as she obviously did, that I was responsible for the terrible state Glacial Stare was in. And whatever Joan had told her about me…and despite everything *she'd* told the doctor…she'd been a nurse long enough to know that even a woman who has been married to a man for many years can never be sure he won't develop some odd, wild quirk of character which will turn him into a murderer overnight.

And that's even more true of a hospital patient who has been close to death and running a fever and may still be in an irresponsible state, his reason undermined by the suffering he's undergone.

And she was completely right about one thing. I was entirely responsible for the terrible state Glacial Stare was in. Only...there had been a reason for the violence I had unleashed against him, and I wanted her to hear the full story as quickly as posssible, so that she would calm down and become a responsible person again herself.

Hysteria is a woman's worst enemy...and a man's too, for that matter. But since it's ten times as common in women as in men it's a very special problem, which every man should know how to deal with. I was no expert at it, but she helped me by listening to what I had to say in my own defense as if her life depended on it. And when I was through she seemed to agree with me that if someone had put an ether cone over Glacial Stare's face in his sleep and relieved him of life's burdens in a painless, merciful way they would have been doing humanity a service.

"It's not right to feel that way," she said. "It makes you wonder about yourself when you even think you'd like to see someone who's that ruthless removed from a world that has too many merciless people in it. But I guess everyone who isn't that way...thinks about it at times."

"I did more than think about it," I said. "But in the main I battered him unconscious just to give myself a one in ten chance of staying alive. The odds against me have shrunk a little, but not much. Unless I can get out of here fast—"

"You can!" she breathed. "I'll help you. No one will try to stop us, if we make it look as if I was just walking with you to the end of the corridor and back. We get patients right out of bed after minor surgery, to keep them from losing their strength. It's the best way."

"Minor surgery! You mean—"

Nurse Cherubin nodded. "They didn't have to probe to get the dart out. It didn't go deep into your back. It was the poison that made you so ill. The dart struck a bone and that jammed the poison mechanism. The dart splintered just a little, but not enough poison got into your bloodstream to kill you. But you ran a fever and once or twice I was really frightened, because your pulse started fluttering and you almost stopped breathing."

"Good God!" I looked at her, wondering. "If I was that close to death how could my strength have come back so fast? I don't feel too good right now. But I had enough strength when I crashed into him to drag him from the chair, lift him up and slam him back against the wall."

She nodded. "Even a dying man can do that sometimes, if he's threatened in a violent enough way and desperately wants to stay alive. But you weren't that weak, and you're not going to die. You've got more strength right now than you realize. And you'll get stronger—not weaker. After minor surgery the post-operative shock is usually minor too, and the fever didn't last long enough to seriously weaken you. The last blood test was good. No poison—not even a millionth of a c.c. You perspired freely, and that helped to save your life."

"All right," I said. "That's good news. Just the fact that you're the only one who knows what would happen if I don't get out of here fast would be better news—the best there is. Except that—"

I shook my head and looked past her toward the door. "What good would a walk up the corridor do me if there's a Wendel agent stationed at the end of it? A doctor might be taken in, but a Wendel agent would wonder why a nurse was helping me to keep my strength up when I could answer questions better flat on my back. He'd come right back into this room with us, to find out what happened."

"There are no Wendel agents anywhere in the hospital," she said. "The hospital would have put up a fight if a Wendel police officer had insisted on questioning you as *he* did—in private. It would have been a losing battle, and we couldn't have held out for very long. By tomorrow an armed guard would have demanded that you be released in Wendel custody and you can't run a hospital in the Colony if you defy the Wendel police to that extent."

I stared at her, amazed. "Then how did he get in here to see me?"

It was then that she exploded the bombshell.

"If the Wendel Combine, with all of its socio-political power, came here in the person of just one man and threatened to make full use of that power if he was not allowed to talk to you in strict privacy...and that man was Henry Wendel himself—"

She shrugged, glancing steadily for a moment at the slumped form of Glacial Stare, with just an uncanny silence hovering over him. No trace now of the power-aura that must have made hundreds of his yes-men turn pale and snap to attention at various times in the past, if the look he'd trained on me was ingrained and habitual with him. And I rather thought it was.

Mr. Big himself! And I'd banged him around without knowing, without even suspecting that I was slamming the Wendel Power Combine back against a hospital-room wall. All the immense height and depth and weight of it, the big atomic transmission lines, the towering black turbines, the boa constrictor coils that snaked in all directions through the center of the Colony. The war, too—the wolf-eat-wolf war that was being waged with Endicott Fuel, and the demoralization that was sounding taps over graves that hadn't been dug yet but would bear the Wendel trademark.

The lawful authority that the silver bird had conferred on me would have given me the right to act as his executioner then and there. But you can't solve problems that way and hope to gain by it...because there are always other Mr. Bigs waiting to step into the shoes of the Mr. Big you've taken care of in behalf of the common wealth, with more cock-sureness than you've any right to exercise.

When you cut off the head of that kind of boa constrictor and leave the big coils intact the new head may be twice or three times as dangerous.

That he had come to the hospital alone, completely unguarded, would have been hard to believe if I hadn't remembered that an attempt had been made to blast the sky ship apart in space solely because Wendel wanted me out of the way. I was sure of that now. And if he wanted me dead that bad, safeguarding his person would probably have seemed of minor importance to him. It could be waived—an inconsequential detail. I had to be questioned and then killed, and he was the best man for the job. He could trust no one else to handle it as well.

The joker was—he had botched it.

There were a lot more questions I wanted to ask Nurse Cherubin but there just wasn't time for them. We'd wasted four or five minutes already, just discussing the state of my health, and at any moment someone might come through the door who would refuse to let me leave when he saw what I'd done to Wendel.

It wouldn't have to be a Wendel agent. No doctor who wasn't keen about committing suicide would have let me go until Wendel came to, and our two stories could be compared. I didn't have the silver bird to back up my story, and when Wendel came to he'd simply step to a tele-communicator and the hospital would be swarming with Wendel agents before I could hope to win any converts. The fact that he'd come to visit me unguarded didn't mean he'd placed himself in any real jeopardy...in his book at least. He couldn't have known I'd knock him out cold, and even if the hospital was located fifteen miles from the Colony it wouldn't take the Wendel police long to get to him. Ten or twelve minutes, at most.

Perhaps they were already on the way. It stood to reason.

He'd hurried himself and arrived ahead of them, but he'd want them to be there as soon as he killed me, to dump my body on a stretcher and carry it out under guard.

When he killed me—God, how easy it was to overlook the most vital things! I hadn't even searched him. If he had a weapon on him I could certainly use it, for nothing can boost your morale quite so much when your life is at stake as the firm, cool feel of an atomic handgun against your palm.

I was starting toward him when Nurse Cherubin said: "Stay here, and keep the door locked until I come back. I'll tap three times. I've got to get you some clothes."

I nodded, feeling overwhelmingly grateful; tempted to take another minute—precious as every minute was—to tell how wonderful I thought her. She seemed to know without my saying a word, for her wide mouth smiled a little and she was gone.

I stepped to the door and locked it, and then returned across the room and bent over Mr. Big.

I found the weapon but I had to roll him over to get at it, because it was in a holster at his hip. His body was a dead weight, but when I got the weapon free he stirred a little and groaned. I clouted him on the jaw and he stopped groaning. Brutal? You bet it was, but I couldn't afford to take any chances on his coming to.

What would you have done? If I'd killed him right then and there, the Board would not have censured me. I was sure of that. Not to have done so was perhaps foolish, a weakness in me. I was cutting down my chances of getting as far as the Colony, before a security alert went out, and the Wendel police started after me with instructions to blast me down on sight.

But somehow I couldn't do it. Not only for the reasons I've mentioned...because a new head on the Wendel boa constrictor would have solved nothing...but because it went against the grain. I'd have had a feeling of guilt I never could have completely thrown off. He'd intended to kill me, all right...no doubt of that. But I couldn't return the compliment in the same coin. It made no sense, perhaps, but that's the way it was.

The weapon pleased me. It was an atomic handgun that had cost a small fortune to construct—intricate, extremely compact, the latest model, the finest, the best. Fortunately I knew a great deal about such weapons, because unusual-type firearms have always fascinated me.

This one I was sure I could aim and fire with accuracy, even though some of the precision gadgetry was new to me. Twenty-five thousand dollars at least that gun had set Henry Wendel back, but what was twenty-five thousand to a man with a fortune of eight or ten billion?

It seemed tragic and a pity that all of that money should have been spent on a weapon that would pass out of his hands into the possession of a man unfriendly to him. But it didn't sadden me too much and I felt even less sad when I'd unbuckled the holster also, strapped it to my own hip and thrust the handgun back into it.

She knocked three times, as she'd promised and came in with some clothes that some poor devil in another room would never live to put on again. She told me as much while I was taking off my one-piece in-patient garment.

"Cancer," she said. "They're keeping him under sedation. You think you're in trouble, that the game is hardly worth the candle, until you see something like that. Then you realize how lucky you are—just to be alive."

"You don't have to tell me," I said. "I've often thought along those lines."

She wasn't embarrassed when I stood for a moment stark naked before her, as most nurses aren't. I wasn't particularly embarrassed either, because right at that moment I had no more sex awareness than a totem pole.

The clothes were a little small for me, but I had a feeling that in the Colony not too much attention was paid to the way clothes fitted you—or failed to fit. In a pioneering society ill-fitting clothes are accepted as an indication that you are a rough-and-tumble sort of guy, know your way around and are, for good measure, an old-timer, with early-settler prestige.

There were two more questions I had to ask her before I became a babe-in-the-woods kind of grown man on Mars, with just the handgun and a few highly trained areas of native intelligence to protect me—if I succeeded in getting out of the hospital alive. It was still a very big *if,* but the questions were just as vital, and were directly tied in with it.

Just how far *was* the hospital from the Colony? And what was she going to tell Joan to keep her from succumbing to panic when my darling wanted to know what had become of me?

Before we left the room she answered the second question reassuringly. It had been weighing so heavily on my mind I'd been afraid to even let myself bring it right out into the open and face it squarely. Mr. Big hadn't even mentioned Joan in the ugly little talk I'd had with him, and if she was still somewhere in the hospital I had a feeling he'd have used her nearness as one more way of tightening the thumbscrew.

I'd been right about that, apparently. "She had a talk with Commander Littlefield on the tele-communicator," Nurse

Cherubin said. "He advised her to return to the Mars' rocket a few hours ago. He wanted to talk to her...said it was urgent...and promised to check on your progress report every half-hour. She left in one of the outgoing ambulances. She told me she'd be back just as soon as you regained consciousness. It's a very short trip in an ambulance. The hospital is only eight miles from the Colony."

So that answered my first question too, but only in part. If there was just a waste of blowing sand outside it would certainly cut down my chances. But there had to be a firm-packed road for the ambulances to travel over, didn't there?

"No," she said, answering me in full a half-minute later, when the door of the hospital room had been firmly closed behind us and we were committed to the big risk and there could be no turning back. She paused an instant to urge me to be cautious, to stagger a little and grip her arm for support and try to look in all respects like a patient taking his first uncertain walk after a minor operation. I didn't have to worry about looking pale, but when she went on and explained what she'd meant by the "no" relief swept over me and probably marred a little the impression it was important to give anyone who chanced to glance our way.

"There's no desert to cross," she said. "It's all built up. You'll be passing between high stone walls with massive metal grills set deep in the stone most of the time, with here and there a gap and a few scattered pre-fabs occupied by aerator-system workers and their families."

So that was it! I knew all about the Martian aerator-system and the big turbines that pumped oxygen out over the Colony. So much oxygen, under such stabilized pressure, that it stayed in equilibrium and didn't fly off into space even under the light gravity. Even without the aerators there was enough oxygen in the thin Martian atmosphere to enable a man to stay alive for a short period, if he didn't mind going about with his shoulders bent, gasping for breath and turning blue at intervals. His cheeks, anyway, with the veins on his forehead standing out like whipcords.

The first colonists, as everyone knows, went about with oxygen tanks strapped to their backs and took a whiff or two of the stuff in Earth-atmosphere concentration through a flexible metal tube whenever their lungs started burning. And inside the early pre-fabs, of course, there were miniature aerator systems which made living indoors as comfortable as it was Earthside.

But the big aerator-system had completely eliminated the need—a health hazard-diminishing need at best and never actually mandatory—of the huge glass dome which imaginative science writers in the first three decades of the Space Age had predicted as a *must* for successful Martian colonization. There are seldom any *musts* when science advances in seven league boots and you're right on the scene in person, breathing in a planet's atmosphere for yourself and finding out that there just happens to be a little more oxygen in it than precision instruments on Earth had led you to anticipate.

It wasn't a precision instrument of any kind I was needing right at that moment—even to reassure me about my heartbeat. I knew exactly how fast it was beating—much too fast. We passed a doctor in a smock so spotless it didn't seem as if he could have been wearing it for longer than a few minutes. But the look of quick suspicion he trained on us was ageless, the kind of look that comes into the eyes of a trained professional man when he can't be quite sure that a subordinate is doing the wise thing.

What right had the nurse to take me for a walk along the corridor when I looked that close to caving in? I feared for an instant I was overdoing the act, but when the suspicion faded and he went past us along the corridor I breathed more freely again. We passed a nurse who didn't even glance at us and another—blonde and pert-nosed—who smiled and nodded, just as if we were old friends. I wondered what she saw in me.

Then we were standing before an elevator at the end of the corridor and the red down light came on…because Nurse Cherubin had pressed the down button…and she was urging me to be cautious for the second time.

"We're going down three flights to the admitting ward," she said. She smiled, as if she'd suddenly remembered there's nothing like a touch of levity to relieve strain, even if it has to be forced. "But don't let that dishearten you. Patients are discharged from the admitting ward too. It's not quite as long as this corridor but it will be busier. Patients, nurses—at least three doctors. We'll just walk right through as if we had every right to be there. Just outside the emergency exit, a few steps further on, there's a driveway, which curves around behind the hospital. Ambulances with accident victims use it, but there's not likely to be an ambulance standing there. You go down a narrow flight of stairs to get to it. Is that clear?"

I nodded. "What do I do then?"

"You just follow the driveway until it forks and the left turn will take you into the clear-away between the aerators which leads directly to the Colony. You won't have to pass in front of the hospital at all. Ambulances may pass you before you get to the Colony, but you won't be stopped and questioned. They'll think you're one of the aeration-system workers."

I had an impulse to give her a hug and tell her I loved her, quite sure that she'd know what I meant, even if I did it inside the elevator where it would have more an aspect of intimacy. You love people who go all out to help you and they don't even have to be young and beautiful. But when they are there's an added warmth somehow—

147

We carried it off better than I'd dared to hope. We descended in the elevator, emerged arm in arm and walked right through the admitting ward without even glancing at the fifteen or twenty people we had to pass to get to the emergency exit she'd mentioned, a third of them in white. No one stopped or questioned us, and we followed the same nurse-helping-patient routine, which had proved its worth on the third floor of the hospital.

And then—I did hug and kiss her, just once briefly before I went out through the exit and down the stairs to the driveway. I hoped Joan wouldn't mind if she ever got to hear about it.

"Goodbye," I said. "And thank you."

## CHAPTER SIXTEEN

THERE WAS NO WAITING AMBULANCE in the driveway. I descended the stairway, twelve metal steps railed in on both sides, feeling grateful for what she'd said right after I kissed her. "Don't worry about your wife. If Wendel tries to make us send for her we'll find a way to roast him over a slow fire until you're together again. There are three doctors who will put up a stiff fight and I'm going to set to work on all of them. You've no idea what a hospital can do with just the right kind of delaying tactics."

It took me less than two minutes to half-encircle the driveway, take the turn she'd recommended and strike out for the Colony between the towering gray walls of the aerators.

The Big Grayness. I'd seen photographs of that tremendous engineering project in my hell-bent-for-adventure years, when I'd sat at a desk in a schoolroom, and imagined what it would be like to take part in the construction work, standing on a dizzy height with an electronic riveter in my hand, watching blue lights go on and off and sparks fly up into the cool Martian night beneath a wilderness of stars.

The reality was very much as I'd imagined it as a school kid, except that I wasn't a construction worker looking down over it, a human fly with a man-size job to do, but a guy that kid wouldn't have recognized, his footsteps echoing on the catwalk at the base of it. I had a giant-size job to do, but how could he have known it would some day turn into anything *that* big?

It wasn't even a project anymore—half of it still in the blueprint stage. It was completed and the towering gray walls were firm and solid, and the grills were sending oxygen spiraling out over the Colony without making me feel light-headed at all.

Right at that moment I'd have welcomed a little oxygen intoxication but the aerator-system didn't work that way. The flow was regulated directly at the source, kept under controlled pressure and diffused outward high up by rotary circulators. As it spread out over the Colony it was drawn down to breathing level by another system of circulators, stationed at intervals about the Colony and extending twenty-five miles out into the surrounding desert.

If you wanted to experience oxygen intoxication you had to strap a tank to your back and breathe the stuff in through a tube in the old way. But no one in his right mind would do that deliberately, for an excess of oxygen can be five-ways dangerous on a planet where what you have to worry about most is over-stimulation.

There were catwalks on both sides of the aerator walls, with a central lane wide enough for vehicles to pass in opposite directions. I kept to the right hand side all the way to the Colony, and it took me about thirty minutes to get there. My strength amazed me. It probably wasn't quite up to par.

But I only had to stop twice to rest and then only for a minute or two.

Two ambulances passed me, their red taillights blinking, but the drivers didn't even turn their heads as the vehicles went droning through the Big Grayness. Up above the sunlight was waning, and turning red, but only a diffuse glow filled that two hundred-foot-high artificial cavern.

Three aerator-system workers, walking shoulder to shoulder, gave me a bad jolt for a moment, for they had the look of Wendel police agents. I encountered them just beyond a break in the cavern wall, where a cluster of pre-fabs with children playing in the yards made five or six acres of stony ground resemble a manufacturing town suburb Earthside.

I should have known better than to be alarmed, because the three men approaching me looked eager and expectant, as if they knew that a few steps more would bring relaxation after toil and the warmth and glow of a family reunion.

But they had the husky build and sharp-angled features of Wendel police officers and I stayed alert until one of them came to a dead halt and looked me over genially. "New on the job, aren't you, Buster? Don't remember having run into you before. They keep putting on so many new men it's hard to be sure."

"That's right," I said. "I live about two miles further on."

"Well, it isn't the best job in the world, Buster, as I guess you've found out already. You get sucked into a grill sometimes, and breathe nothing but oxygen until you feel like a blue baby they're trying their best to save, even if they have to fanny-whack him to get the stuff out of his lungs for a week or two afterwards."

"Don't discourage him, Pete," the tallest of the three chided. "You have a cold, cold heart. It doesn't happen often."

"You bet it doesn't…or my wife would have been a widow long before this. Well…good luck, Buster. Be seeing you around…I hope."

I felt so relieved I didn't even resent the "Buster." He was just a big grinning ape who liked to kid the living daylights out of his fellow workers, whenever he thought he could get away with it. No harm in him, and though there might have been times when I'd have been tempted to take a poke at him…I had no such impulse now. I just wanted to be able to look back and see him dwindling in the distance.

I ran into only one other person before the Big Grayness terminated. She was a stout, matronly-looking woman carrying a baby and she nodded and smiled warmly when she saw me staring at the infant, as if she wouldn't have at all minded if I had been its father.

For an instant there flashed into my mind the nerve-relaxing picture that every normal male has of himself at times—the humble-station husband, big-bosomed wife picture. You're Mr. Run-of-the-Mill, just a simple guy, working hard at a lathe or feeding processed food tins into a vacuumator. You come home at night with no worries, kick off your shoes and she's there to make the creature comforts seem important. A good meal on the table, fit for a king with a hearty appetite—do kings ever have that kind of appetite?—children romping all over the house—a round half-dozen upstairs and down—and the kind of night's sleep you don't get when you have responsibilities weighing on you. The top-echelon kind that can drive you half out of your mind. It's there for the taking if you really want it, if you don't wear a silver bird on your uniform when they add up the score and ask you why in hell you haven't done better?

It's not quite an accurate picture, because that kind of guy has worries too—plenty of them. He has to buy shoes for the children and grin and be tolerant when his wife turns shrewish, as every woman with a large family and a big grocery bill is bound to do at times. But still, when you balance the good against the bad, who gets the most out of life—Mr. Run-of-the-Mill or Mr. Big?

Well…however much I might fume about it…I had to be what I was. I could honestly say that I'd never had any driving ambition to be the kind of Mr. Big Wendel was. I just had a kind of inner compulsion to be true to the best that was in me, to preserve my integrity and use whatever wild talents I had to enrich human life and have some fun while doing it. If I couldn't always have fun, if illness or death or just plain bad luck prevented me from living life to the full and enjoying it…I'd known that when I'd cut the cards, hadn't I? You have to play whatever cards destiny hands you.

Just before I reached the last quarter mile of the aerator marathon I passed another dwelling section, with more kids scampering about and three or four women standing in the doorways of the pre-fabs. They didn't look big bosomy, but slender as willow trees and very beautiful.

I certainly wasn't running, but it was a marathon in my book, the walking kind where you keep your body held rigid, your arms bent sharply at the elbows. There was only one good thing about it. I didn't have to worry about out-distancing the other walkers, because it was a one-man marathon.

I came out into the biggest square I'd ever seen. The one opposite the skyport I'd crossed with just as much tension and uncertainty mounting in me an eternity ago on Earth was just about one-fourth as large, give or take a few square yards of shadowy pavement.

In a way, the Big Grayness was still with me, because there were gigantic, interlocking shadows everywhere and although there was nothing but open sky overhead, spirals of wind-blown sand were swirling across it, half-blotting out the waning sunlight.

When you're sure that Death hasn't played his final trump or even relaxed his vigilance and you could be yanked right back to confront him at any moment a square as big and empty and desolate-looking as that doesn't give you any support at all.

All right, there was life and movement in it, if you want to call a long line of tractors standing end to end on the far side, one of them snail-active, life and movement.

One of the trucks seemed to be backing up a little and edging out from between the others, but I couldn't even be sure of that before an ear-splitting blast of sound and a blinding flash of light shattered my last link with the sane universe.

## CHAPTER SEVENTEEN

I WAS LIFTED UP AND HURLED backwards, so violently that if blind luck hadn't saved me I'd have fractured my skull or felt, ripping through my chest, the beaten-drum agony that sets in right after you've shaken hands with a spinal concussion.

I came down heavily, hitting the pavement with a thud. But in falling I went into a kind of half-spin, and landed on my side in a loose-jointed sprawl that just shook me up a little.

I rolled over on my back and stared up in horror. For an instant I was sure that the whole sky had burst into flame. Then the flare dimmed and vanished and I could see that the dust spirals were still there.

I raised myself on one elbow and stared out across the square. The long line of tractors was still there, too. Not one of the vehicles had been blown sky high. And as if that wasn't enough of a miracle the snail-paced one had turned about and was heading straight in my direction.

It wasn't moving at a snail's pace now. It was coming directly at me from mid-way in the square, rumbling and clattering as it came, its heavy treads so ponderously in motion that the pavement under me was beginning to vibrate.

Nearer it came and nearer, swaying a little, and if the driver had been some crazy killer bent on crushing me to death under the treads he couldn't have gone about it more expertly, for he was maneuvering the vehicle just enough to make sure that it would pass directly over me.

How could I doubt it? It had veered slightly and swung back into a straight-line course again, and if I'd tried to drag myself out of its path there was room enough for it to veer again before I could hope to save myself.

It takes several seconds to recover from a scare like that, even when the danger evaporates right before your eyes. All at once the tractor *was* veering again, but far enough to the left to make me feel certain that I wouldn't be flattened to a pancake if I stayed where I was. But you can feel certain about something like that and go right on remembering what big tractors have done at various times in the past to men unfortunate enough to be caught off guard when there's a killer in the driver's seat.

The vehicle came to a jolting, grinding halt a few yards to the left of me, and the driver swung himself out of the glass-shielded front seat, descended lightly to the ground, and was grabbing me by the arm and helping me to rise before I could get a really good look at him.

He'd descended from the tractor lightly because he was that kind of a man—just about the most fragile-looking guy I'd ever seen. He was lean to the point of emaciation, with gaunt cheeks and sparse white hair that was fluffed out like thistledown by the wind that was blowing across the square.

He had deep set brown eyes, very sharp and piercing and they were glowing now with a kind of feverish brightness, as if his agitation matched my own or had reached a peak that was just a trifle higher. There was nothing surprising about that, if he knew exactly what had happened and it was as bad as I feared it might be.

Despite his frailness, he had the features of a strong-willed man, the chin and mouth firm, the nose pinched a little at the nostrils, as if stubbornness in adversity had become an ingrained habit with him. I had the feeling I'd seen that face before, but I couldn't remember where or under what circumstances.

I was certainly seeing it now under the most nerve shattering of all circumstances and would not be likely to forget it a second time.

"How are you, all right?" he asked, his eyes searching my face as if he was far from sure I knew myself and the way I looked would tell him more than just a guess on my part. "That explosion was miles from here," he went on breathlessly, "but it lifted the tractor right off the ground, treads and all, for a second. I had the craziest kind of floating sensation until it settled down and kept right on in this direction. I increased the speed, because I sort of felt that a fast-moving machine would have a better chance of not overturning."

I stared at him half-dazedly, feeling like a pawn on a chessboard that had tilted just far enough to make me wonder if it might not still be precariously poised and go crashing at any moment. And since I couldn't see the players I didn't know what the rules of that particular game were or how far they had been abrogated.

"How do you feel?" he asked.

His solicitude amazed me, because if what he'd just said was true—and I had no reason to doubt it—he should have been more shaken up than I was and he seemed to have something on his mind that was making him stare straight past me toward the Big Grayness.

I was staring in the opposite direction. "I'm all right," I assured him. "Just feel…a little dizzy." I gestured toward the tractors on the far side of the square. "What's over there? Did the explosion come from there?"

He shook his head. "No. I told you it was miles from here, in the direction of the spaceport. That's the Endicott Administration Building, fuel conveyor sections and two-thirds of the distributing units. The tractors are all owned by Endicott. I backed this one out from between them and had just about gotten it turned around when the blast hit me."

"I know," I said. "I saw you. I wondered why only one tractor—"

That was as far as I got, because what hit me then was more jolting than any blast could have been, and it wasn't even physical. Just one word he'd let drop with a delayed-action fuse attached to it made me snap my head back and look at him in desperation. He had no way of knowing what was in my mind, but you don't think of that when you want someone to do you a favor that's of life-and-death importance to you.

I wanted him to withdraw that one word, to pretend at least that he hadn't said it. It didn't have to be true, he could have been just guessing.

The word was "spaceport." It couldn't matter that much to him, surely. It wasn't his wife but mine who was at the spaceport, and if he was wrong about where the explosion had taken place it would cost him nothing to be merciful and admit that he was far from sure about it.

But before I could hope to get such an admission out of him he sounded a knell to the granting of favors by saying: "Wendel technicians are activating Endicott fuel cylinders in different sections of the Colony. They're trying to turn the Colonists against Endicott by committing mass murder. The cylinders will only destroy an area of a few square miles, because they're not in the multiple-megaton, nuclear warhead category. We never thought they'd be turned into bombs."

Then came the knell. "We were warned about this, by a Colonist who's on his way to the spaceport with one of the cylinders. Or he may be there already. He just spoke to us briefly on the tele-communicator. That explosion came from the direction of the spaceport, but it may not be the one we were warned about. They may be trying to dismantle another cylinder at the spaceport right now. They won't succeed, because only an Endicott technician would know how to go about it."

"Do you know?"

He nodded. "Yes…I can dismantle it. I can get to the spaceport in about fifteen minutes, if I drive between the aerators and turn right just before I get to the hospital. The clear-away from that point on will take me through a section of the Colony and then straight out across the desert to the spaceport. The Colonist who talked with us made a serious mistake, but it wasn't his fault. He had no way of knowing that it takes a fuel cylinder at least forty-five minutes to build up to critical mass after it's been activated. In some cases—fifty or fifty-five minutes."

He paused an instant, then went on quickly. "He should have brought it here. We could have dismantled it in time. But he was afraid it would kill several thousand people if it went off anywhere near his home, or in this section of the Colony. He also over-estimated the area that would be demolished by the blast. When he talked to us he was two-thirds of the way to the spaceport and if we'd told him to turn back then and bring the cylinder here the risks would have been too great. We had to let him go on. I said they can't dismantle it at the spaceport. But there's a slim chance they can…because there may be an Endicott man there or someone who knows enough about Endicott cylinders to make a hit-or-miss try. With luck, he may just possibly succeed. But I doubt it."

"You doubt it? Good God—"

"I doubt it very much. That's why it's so important for me to get there as fast as I can. It's my responsibility—and I refuse to share it with anyone. There are times when a man must face death alone."

"Who are you?" I asked.

"A man with much to answer for, the opposite of a good man. I'm Kenneth H. Hillard, President of the Endicott Combine."

It stunned me for a moment, because it was as big a bombshell as Nurse Cherubin had exploded back at the hospital when she'd nodded toward a slumped caricature of a man and told me exactly whom I'd been banging around.

But it didn't stun me for long, because even the showdown miracle of two Mr. Big's taking matters into their own hands when all of the chips were down—Hillard was also a giant despite his frailness and a better man than Wendel could ever hope to be—even the wonder and strangeness of it was of less concern to me at that moment than the danger that Joan was in.

I told him then. "I'm going with you," I said. "I've every right. If I'm cutting in on your yen to face death alone…that's just too bad. I'm going with you, or you don't go at all. I pack quite a wallop, and you may as well know it. Wendel does."

"Your wife. I see…"

"I hope to Christ you do—"

"Get in!" he said sharply. "I may need you. I'm not a well man. My heart—"

We climbed in and he tugged at the brakes, releasing them and the big vehicle lumbered into motion.

It was already pointed in the right direction, and in less than half a minute—the second time within fifteen minutes for me—we were deep in the Big Grayness, with the walls of the aerators looming up on both sides of us.

Up above all of the sunlight had dwindled to the vanishing point and the gigantic artificial cavern was lighted now along its entire length by cold light lamps embedded in the walls at fifty-foot intervals. The solid, three-dimensional world outside our minds, whatever segment of reality we happen to be passing through, never looks quite the same to any two individuals. It is always, in a sense, a special creation, colored and altered by the human imagination.

To me the cold light lamps were chillingly like enormous eyes, keeping us under constant scrutiny. The scrutiny of giants, standing motionless in shadows, with just their luminous eye-sockets visible. It was as if any moment, promoted by some wild whim, the giant forms might take a violent dislike to us, might raise mace-like metal fists and smash the tractor, very much as a robot giant had smashed a Wendel agent in space, with a fiendishly mechanical rancor.

But to the frail man at my side the aerator walls may have been chilling in a quite different way, if he was giving the Big Grayness any thought at all.

Apparently he wasn't, because when his voice rose above the rumble of the treads he didn't once mention the aerators or the pale blue light that was glimmering on the hood of the tractor.

"It's the beginning of the end—either one way or the other," he shouted. "Either Wendel will be destroyed by the

Colonists themselves for committing mass murder, or we'll go down under a juggernaut that can't be stopped. Sometimes you can't smash absolute evil, when it's backed up by absolute power."

I raised my voice as high as he'd done, because I wanted to be sure he'd hear me. "It will always be stopped in the end, I think—if you have enough moral courage. That's a dynamic in itself, the most formidable of all weapons. All history confirms it."

"I wish I could believe that!" he shouted back. "But I'm not so sure. And you have to fight with reasonably clean hands. Endicott is almost as guilty as Wendel, except that it would rather be destroyed than resort to mass murder."

"That's two-thirds of the right," I shouted back. "That's where the biggest dividing line comes. Every tyranny in human history that has resorted to mass murder has gone down into everlasting night and darkness and very quickly. The few that survived to die a natural death drew back at that point. The great, utterly ruthless destroyers always perish."

We both fell silent then, because there are times when the whole of the future and everything that human anger and courage can do to safeguard the future and keep it from destruction seems less important than coming to grips with an immediate, life-and-death emergency. When you do that you're going all out to safeguard the future as well, but you don't think of it in that way. Just getting to the spaceport in time—Oh, God, yes, in time to be at least a little ahead of time, so that Hillard would have steady nerves and could dismantle the cylinder with cautious precision, with no zero-count demoralization to make his fingers stray from the right wires—just getting there and finishing the job before the spaceport could become a translucent cone of fire was a million times as important to me, right at that moment, as the Wendel-Endicott war.

A million times as important, Ralphie boy. Don't be ashamed of feeling that way. If the spaceport blows up, and there's no Joan any more, and the universe comes to an end for you, you've no sure guarantee that the actors who will step into your shoes and occupy the center of the stage will make any better job of it than you've been doing. So it will be a loss, however you slice it, because the death of two lovers is always a loss. You fight better when you've been given that best of all head starts.

## CHAPTER EIGHTEEN

WE STAYED SILENT UNTIL THE TRACTOR had rumbled past eight or ten of the breaks in the Big Grayness. They were shrouded in dusk-light now, with no kids playing in the front yards of the housing area pre-fabs. Then, just as we were turning into the clear-away that branched off from the one I'd taken on leaving the hospital Hillard shouted: "We've got to get over to the left! There's an ambulance right up ahead!"

I heard the siren before I saw it, a banshee-like wail cutting through the twilight, unnerving in its shrillness. It took a moment or two for its winking red headlights to come sweeping toward us and if Hillard had seen them before that it had to mean he had exceptionally sharp eyesight.

It careened past without slowing, almost grazing the hood of the tractor. I thought for an instant, when the banshee wail became shrill again, that it was still coming from the same ambulance. Then I saw four more furiously blinking headlights coming out of the dusk ahead of us, and another ambulance swept past, as swiftly as the first had done, but missing us by a wider margin.

A third followed it at a distance of less than a hundred feet, its siren at such full blast that it no longer sounded like a banshee wail.

You can be gripped by a dread that's practically breath stopping and still manage to shout, if your only other choice is to die inwardly.

It may have been more of a groan than a shout. My voice sounded ragged and it almost broke. "Could those ambulances be coming from the spaceport? Do you think-"

He cut me off. I probably couldn't have gone on anyway.

"They could never have gotten out there and back so fast!" he shouted. "We'll be passing through a section of the Colony in about two more minutes. It's closer to the hospital, so it's just possible they've picked up a few victims at the fringe of the blast area who didn't have our luck."

"The fallout area must be pretty wide!" I shouted back. "Wherever the explosion took place—"

He cut me off again. "No fallout—or very little. What there is is gone within four or five minutes. Safe to go in after that, for the residue wouldn't mutate a fruit fly. Colonists don't know that...closely guarded Endicott trade secret. Reason we let the Colonists store them. A fuel cylinder can be converted into a nuclear bomb, all right, but it will be the cleanest midget bomb ever built. Take fifteen or twenty of them to blow up even a third of the Colony. But that doesn't mean that one couldn't blow up the spaceport, or seriously injure hundreds of people throughout the fringe area. The ground tremor alone could do that. I told you what it did to this tractor. Has the force of a small earthquake, except that the tremors are three times as erratic. They can just shake you up a little, or break every bone in your body. Depends on where you happen to be standing. It follows a zigzagging pattern, so it can pass right by you."

All that didn't come in one shout, but I'm recording it that way because I didn't interrupt him, and though he must have stopped once or twice to take a deep breath, and keep a sharp lookout for another ambulance I wasn't aware of any break in what he was saying. He was trying his best to make it crystal clear, if only to calm me down a little.

Some of it was reassuring, but not what he'd said about the spaceport. A clean bomb with little or no fallout can leave you just as dead if you're unfortunate enough to be blown up by it. You see things sometimes you can't bring yourself to talk about, even to close friends when the horror has receded a little and you know it can't come back in a physical way to torment you.

So I'm going to draw the veil over most of what we saw when we passed through about five square miles of the Colony, before the clear-away broadened out to twice its previous width and we headed out across the desert toward the spaceport.

We couldn't be sure, even then, just where the explosion had taken place, because it was only the fringe area we passed through. It hadn't been laid waste by the blast and there were only five or six demolished buildings. If the big square, which stretched between the Endicott plant and the aerators, had been a built-up section instead of a square the property damage might have been just as great and would not have seemed ruinous.

But there was one other difference. The Endicott square had been unpopulated, with just one tractor moving out from the long line of tractors on the far side. The five miles of Colony we passed through had been the opposite of unpopulated. Its streets and squares and playgrounds and vehicle-parking areas had been thronged with people.

They were still thronged with people but some of them were lying prone, and others were leaning dazedly against the walls of buildings which had remained for the most part undamaged and still others, who no longer seemed to be in a state of shock, were bending over the slumped bodies of the grievously injured and the dying, doing their best to console them and ease their pain.

I'm drawing the veil on the rest of it—the blood and the screaming—because it was pretty awful, and what possible purpose would be served if I described it? How could it benefit anyone? It would serve as a reminder of how cruel life can be at times, how uncertain and terrible. We know that, don't we? So…to hell with it…I say that in a very reverent way, with awe and respect, and not profanely. But it's best to consign it where it belongs, to hell, and not let it paralyze all action and make you give up when there are still sunsets, and the laughter of children, and the happiness of lovers, and ten thousand other things that are worth fighting to preserve.

It took us less than eight minutes to arrive at the spaceport, dusty from head to foot, with sand choking our lungs and gasping a little from oxygen shortage, because when there's a stiff wind blowing over the desert the aerators don't function at peak efficiency.

I didn't know there was anything wrong until the tractor began to zigzag a little, about three hundred feet from the massive, steel-mesh gates of the spaceport.

He had strength enough left to tug at the brakes and bring the tractor to a grinding halt before he slumped against me, with a strangled sob that chilled me to the core of my being. It chilled me and stunned me and frightened me, because I'd never thought that anything like that could happen.

He was frail, all right, and had the look of a man whose health had been steadily failing…no doubt partly brought about by the battle he'd been waging with Wendel. And he'd mentioned something about heart-trouble—

The trouble was, I hadn't taken all that too seriously, because you never think that someone who has displayed extraordinary energy and firmness of will is going to collapse right when you need him most.

I swung about and looked at him, and his pallor gave me an even worse jolt than the way he'd moaned and sagged heavily against me.

He gripped my arm and tried to speak, but the words wouldn't come. His lips moved soundlessly for a moment and then—they stopped moving. His body stopped moving too. All at once, as if a clock had stopped ticking inside of him, and Time had stopped ticking for him forever just because his life and the clock were bound up together, intricate parts of the same mechanism, and if the clock stopped there was no way his life could be prolonged.

I knew he was dead before I reached out and touched him. I could tell by the dull, unseeing glaze, which had overspread his pupils, and the terrible stillness that had come upon him. A stillness and a rigidity that made it impossible for me to doubt what the alarm bells were telling me as well. They had started ringing again, but this time it wasn't so much an alarm they were sounding as a dirge.

It was impossible for me to doubt, but I still had to make sure, as he would have wanted me to do, by feeling for a heartbeat that wasn't there and satisfying myself in other ways. It was an obligation I couldn't evade and had no intention of evading.

It took me less than a minute and a half—a time limit I kept firmly in mind—to fulfill that obligation. Then I descended from the tractor and headed for the steel-mesh gates of the spaceport on the run.

# CHAPTER NINETEEN

"RALPH!" SHE CRIED, RUNNING TO MEET me as I walked into the big, steel-walled enclosure where Commander Littlefield and eight or ten or possibly twelve men in gray skyport-technician uniforms were working over a long metal cylinder that Death had started working on well ahead of them. He was the expert and they were just amateurs doing the best they could to beat the time limit he had set for them. With a grim chuckle, no doubt, because, as I said once before, Death is a weird-o.

Joan's arms went around my shoulders and she crushed herself against me, and kissed me hard on the mouth. Then she let go of me and moved quickly to one side, so that Commander Littlefield could talk to me without interference or a moment's delay. She seemed to know without waiting for me to say a word how important that was.

One look at Littlefield's white face told me all I really wanted to know. But I decided that if he could fill in the details for me in half a minute I could risk setting another time limit in my mind and clocking him second by second by second as he talked.

"A nurse at the hospital got word to us you'd be doing your best to get back here, Ralph," he said. "The Wendel police have orders to blast you down on sight, but now that you're here I can protect you—or you can protect yourself. I've got your papers and insignia. Right now that's not so urgent as what's happening inside this Endicott fuel cylinder. It's been triggered to build up to critical mass by a Wendel agent. A Colonist brought it here and we've been trying to dismantle it. But we don't know just how to go about it and we don't dare experiment. We've taken a few *small* risks, naturally. We've had to. But we're getting nowhere, and what looks like a small risk could turn out to be a big one. We don't even know how much time we've got!"

He spoke almost calmly, without raising his voice, but there was nothing calm about the way he looked. The time limit I'd set to clock him by had run out and now it was my turn. I was going to have to ask him to do something that might seem only a little less terrible to him than being blown apart by a nuclear explosion.

But it would have to be done—and fast.

I clocked myself as I talked, allowing myself about forty seconds. "Those cylinders build up to critical mass when they've been tampered with and triggered to explode in about forty-five minutes," I said. "Don't ask me how I know, because I haven't time to explain. I *do* know—you can take my word for it. I knew the cylinder was here, and I was hoping you'd find a way—"

I caught myself up. "Never mind that now. Just listen. I don't know how long it took the Colonist to bring it here or how long you've been working over it. But it hasn't exploded yet. *So there's still a chance we can get it out into space before it blows up!*"

He looked at me as if he thought I'd gone suddenly quite mad. I finished what I had to say fast, because I knew it would take eight or ten more minutes for him to recover from his first shock, and issue orders, and have the cylinder carried on board his big sky ship—his pride and glory—and for the sky ship to rise from its launching pad and be blown apart in space.

He'd have to get all of the crewmen off as well and set the robot controls and if there were any passengers still on board—I refused to let myself think about that.

"It may be too late," I went on. "We may all be as good as dead right now. But we've got to try. Do you understand? You've got to get that cylinder on the sky ship, set the controls and send it out into space. *It must be done at once. Every second counts.*"

He recovered from the shock faster than I'd dared to hope. The grin that hovered for the barest instant on his lips startled me until I realized it was a very special kind of grin— the kind of grin only a man who is about to part with something that means just about as much to him as his own life would be capable of…if he had a non-eradicable streak of wry humor deep in his nature as well.

"Ralph, I've always looked upon people who put property above human life as just about the lowest worms that crawl. But for a minute—God pity me—I almost felt that way. It's just that—it's fifty billion dollars worth of big, tremendous sky ship and that cylinder is so small—"

"It won't seem small if it blows up and takes the spaceport with it," I said. "It won't seem small at all."

"I know, Ralph. I said once I was old enough to be your father and I still think I am. But if you put me across your knee and gave me the drubbing a dumb six-year-old would rate I'd have no right to complain. I should have thought of it myself."

"We don't always think of things that stand out like sore thumbs when we're under tremendous stress," I said. "Don't blame yourself for being human, Commander."

"I hope it won't take me much longer than that to finish the job, Ralph," he said. "I'll do my best. There are only three crewmen on board and all of the passengers have been cleared."

He swung about without another word and went striding out of the enclosure.

I would have followed him if Joan hadn't picked that moment to come back into my arms. It held me up for a minute or two.

The incandescent burst of flame that makes a big sky ship's ascent into space seem for an instant almost cataclysmic, as if the sky itself had been ripped apart in some terrible and incomprehensible way, came exactly eight minutes, thirty-two seconds later.

I timed it myself, not mentally this time but with a watch in my hand. I stood with Joan at my side a hundred feet from the launching pad, watching the cylinder disappear into the sky. It was the cylinder and not the big rocket itself that I seemed to see as I stared upward, as if the sky ship had turned to glass and the deadly thing it was carrying out into space was beginning to stir and vibrate in a quite ghastly way, with its contours enlarged to sky-spanning dimensions under the glass.

To my inward vision it was bigger than the ship itself and it was hard to understand how even a huge sky ship could be carrying anything so enormous and death-freighted when a short while before it had been discharging passengers in the bright Martian sunlight who had given no thought to Death...only what life had in store for them on a new world.

My fingers were clenched around the watch and I wasn't even aware that Commander Littlefield had joined me until he tapped me on the arm.

"We can see and hear it when it happens—all of it, just as if we were taking it out into space ourselves. Every tele-communicator on the sky ship is turned on and tuned to big screen wave length. If there was a crewman on board he could talk to us and we could talk to him."

"Thank God there isn't a living man on board," I breathed.

"Yes," he said, nodding. "Yes, we can be thankful for that. And for our lives as well. There are four big screens here, but we may as well watch the one in the port clearance building. It's the largest of the four—if size makes any difference when about all we'll see when the cylinder explodes is a blinding flare. We won't see the bulkheads collapsing, or a robot cyb crumbling, that's for sure. It will happen too fast."

"What good will it do us to watch at all?" Joan asked. "I'd rather stay right here. We'll see the flash, won't we?"

"You'll see it, all right," Littlefield said, grimly. "It will look like an exploding star for about ten seconds. My sky ship—an exploding star. I never thought it would ever come to that."

He started to turn away, thinking, no doubt, that I'd fallen in with Joan's idea of passing up a view of it on the screen. But I hadn't at all and when he started walking toward the port clearance building I was right at his side. So was Joan, because she was that kind of a wife. There were a lot of questions I wanted to ask him—questions of the utmost urgency, such as how much progress he'd made in finding out who had shot the dart at me from high up on the spiral and just what news he'd received from the hospital, when Nurse Cherubin had informed him I was trying to get back to the spaceport, that went beyond that bare statement—I was sure she'd briefed him in detail—and…well, a lot of questions. But this hardly seemed the right time to ask him, because his inner torment was too great.

I could sympathize and understand, because I knew what a hell he was passing through. Nothing could prevent the destruction of his sky ship, but he had to see it with his own eyes, no matter how much agony it caused him.

He didn't have to do any explaining to the Port Clearance men, because they'd either assumed he'd pick out their screen well in advance of our arrival or their own curiosity had proved overmastering.

The screen was lighted and the sound tracks whirring when we walked into the projection room. It was just like walking into the sky ship's chart room and staring across it at the four robot giants who had followed both emergency instructions in space and the routine kind and were doing their best to perform a man's job now. A mechanical best, which meant, of course, that they had no way of knowing how close they were to annihilation. They would be blown apart without pain and had nothing to lose that a man would have valued. But they were not men, and who can be sure that mechanical brains and the thought processes, which take place in them, are not faintly tinged with emotional coloration?

Probably not...for it would have been something that laboratory tests have never succeeded in establishing. A cybernetic brain can become fatigued, yes—but it is not really a human fatigue. It is on the mental-fatigue level. But knowing all that, a chill would have gone through me if the robots had been able to talk to us.

The image on the screen was three-dimensional, and in full color and the illusion that we were standing right in the sky ship's chart room was so startling that Joan whispered: "I wish we'd stayed outside. It's terrifying. Almost as if...we could be blown up ourselves when the blast comes."

"No danger of that," I said, squeezing her hand reassuringly. "You'd better sit down."

There were ten hollow-tubed metal chairs in the room, but all except one were occupied. I reached out and drew it toward her, but she shook her head. "No, I'll stand, Ralph. I may want to leave in a minute."

One of the port clearance lads got up and offered Commander Littlefield his chair, assuming I'd take the one that Joan had refused. But we were both of one mind about standing. Only Littlefield sat down, as if the burden of torment, which rested upon him, had added ten years to his age.

No sound at all came from the screen for a full minute. Then a scream broke the stillness. It was so totally unexpected, so horrifying, that two of the port clearance men leapt to their feet, sending their chairs spinning backwards. Commander Littlefield was on his feet too, but he hadn't leapt up. He'd arisen jerkily, his hands pressed to his temples, as if to shut out the sound or keep his head from bursting.

We saw her then. She had come into the chart room and was staring directly at us, and just knowing she could see us as clearly as we could see her made her plight seem even more terrible. To me, at least, because it wasn't hard to imagine what was passing through her mind.

*I'm alone on the ship...just as I feared. They've sent me out alone into space. If Commander Littlefield isn't on board...if he's in that room watching me with all those other men...what else can it mean?*

She'd be ten times as sure of it if she'd been inside the port clearance projection room and knew what it looked like, and I was almost certain she had, because there was an unmistakable look of recognition in her eyes, and the Port Clearance building was where they took passengers for questioning.

## CHAPTER TWENTY

SHE LOOKED AS SHE ALWAYS HAD, WITH her hair piled up high on her head and the full lips drowsily sensuous, and her breasts thrusting firmly upward against the tight-clinging fabric that ensheathed them just below the curve of her throat, and the soft whiteness of her upper bosom.

Only her eyes had changed. Stark terror looked out of them and suddenly as she stared at us she pressed one hand to her throat and swayed back against the bulkhead on the right side of the doorway. It brought her up short. But I was sure that if it hadn't she'd have gone right on retreating backwards until she either started screaming again or crumpled to the floor in a dead faint.

She neither screamed again nor fainted, for Commander Littlefield gave her no time to succumb to utter panic. But if his voice hadn't rung out as sharply as it did—at the precise moment that it did—the outcome might have been quite different.

"Why did you return to the ship?" he shouted. "Why did you do such a reckless thing? Was it because we suspected you? Was it because you knew we were about to place you under arrest? Answer me! Your life may depend on it."

"Yes...I went back," she said. "But only to get...something I didn't want you to find. I was pretty sure I'd hidden it where you'd never think of searching, but when you started suspecting me—"

"I see. A damaging piece of evidence? Something of the sort?"

She nodded. "Yes...yes...a paper. It would have proven my guilt."

"You admit your guilt then? We can still save you, but not if you go on lying, clinging to the story you told us. Every part of that is false."

"No, no!" She almost screamed the words. "Most of what I told you was true. My brother did work for Wendel and...I didn't know that he had died. I just found that out a few hours ago. I came to Mars to help him, to save him if I could. I was a Wendel agent, but only because I had no choice. They threatened to kill my brother...used that as a weapon to make me spy for them and do—uglier things."

Her voice rose pleadingly. "Bring the ship back. Don't send me out alone into space. You can't be that cruel—"

"We can't bring the ship back. But we can save you. Just tell the truth. Wendel knew that the Board was sending someone to Mars to investigate the combine, a man who couldn't be bribed to shut his eyes to what he was sure to see here. You had instructions to kill that man before he could set foot on Mars. Wendel wanted him killed because they knew the Board was backing him to the hilt and he had been given enough authority to make him the most dangerous kind of adversary. Wendel also knew that you were the most resourceful and intelligent agent in their employ.

"You proved that, to my satisfaction, when you did what no one has ever done before—outwitted a Mars' rocket security alert system by concealing yourself in a cybernetic robot. I'm sure it didn't take Wendel long to discover that you are as intelligent as you are beautiful—both valuable assets in a secret agent. Priceless assets. The time is very short. Am I right so far?"

"Yes…it's all true. Please…help me!"

"You tried to kill, without success, the man the Board was sending to Mars to investigate and crack down on both Wendel and Endicott. You tried to kill him three times."

"No, only once. I'm telling you the truth. I didn't fire that dart. There were other Wendel agents on board. One tried to blow up the ship. And there were other Wendel agents in New Chicago, with instructions to assassinate him if they could."

"I see. But you did try to kill him in New Chicago. Why did you come to Mars, if you didn't intend to try again?"

"I told you. I didn't lie when I said I came to save my brother, that I wanted to see Wendel exposed…forced to face criminal charges. When I tried to stab him in the New Chicago Underground and failed…I realized what Wendel had done to me, what a vicious person I'd become. I decided I couldn't go on being that kind of person any longer, not even to save my brother. I took the only other way I could think of to keep Wendel from killing my brother. I *am* a resourceful woman, I *am* intelligent…why should I deny it? I might have made the Wendel Combine think twice about killing him. But now my brother's dead and—"

Her shoulders sagged and a look of torment came into her eyes.

"All right. One thing more. When that Wendel agent surprised you in the chart room and the man you'd tried to kill saved you…why were you so frightened? Why did the agent go into such a rage? You must have thought he intended to kill you. And if you were both Wendel agents—"

"I wasn't supposed to be on the ship. He knew it, and must have been pretty sure I'd turned traitor. He knew all about my brother. There wasn't much he didn't know about me, because he was a very high-placed agent. He knew I had every reason to hate Wendel. And I think he was also the kind of man who turns sadistic when he has a woman completely at his mercy."

She saw me then. I could tell by the way her eyes widened and then fastened on me, staring straight past Littlefield as if he was no longer her only accuser.

But she was mistaken if she thought I had any desire to accuse her. I was furious with Littlefield, sickened by his relentless attack on her and if I hadn't been stunned for a moment, caught up in a kind of hypnotic spell by the suddenness of that attack and the startling candor she'd displayed in replying to it I'd have interfered sooner.

What she'd told him was evidence. It would help me to smash Wendel in a legal way, which is always the best way, when backed up as it would have to be by armed, completely lawful authority. All I'd have to do would be to put what she'd just said into one package and what Wendel agents had done to an Endicott fuel cylinder in a densely populated section of the Colony in another and bring the two packages together and there would take place, on Earth and on Mars, the kind of explosion that would blow the Wendel Combine into the rubbish bin of history. The Wendel-Endicott war would be over, and the Colonists would have a new birth of freedom.

A deathbed confession has the strongest kind of legal validity and when a woman thinks she has been sent out into space on an unmanned rocket perhaps to die...she is not likely to lie about anything. An unforeseeable accident—a blind fluke of circumstance—had dealt Littlefield a winning hand and he had taken full advantage of it. He had done it to help me, God pity him...for I hated him for it.

Every question he'd asked her and every reply she'd taken a minute or two to make explicit had cut down her chances of staying on this side of eternity.

She was looking straight at me.

"Ralph!" she said. "I don't want to die alone in space! What are they trying to do to me?"

It was as much as I could take.

I grabbed Littlefield by the shoulders and swung him about and demanded. "You said you could save her. How? Were you lying? If you were...I'll kill you."

"Let go of me, Ralph," he said. "A chance like that would never come again. I had to risk it."

"All right—you've risked it. Now...can you save her? That's all I want to know. Nothing else matters."

"Yes...I think so. If the cylinder doesn't blow up for three or four more minutes. If she puts on a vacuum suit and goes out into space and we're able to pick her up tomorrow or the next day—"

"Then for God's sake tell her. You'll have to tell her about the cylinder, or she won't know how great the danger is. She may take her time about it."

"All right," he said. "I'll take care of it."

He was talking to her in the big screen when Joan and I walked out of the port clearance building.

We walked out because, if the explosion had come while he was talking, just watching it would have killed me. No worse death can come to a man than the one that can take place inwardly, for it can shrivel and blacken his soul and leave him a burnt-out shell of a man until he dies physically. And Joan could sense that, and wanted to get me out of there as quickly as possible.

The explosion came a full ten minutes later, which meant that even Hillard hadn't known how variable the critical mass buildup could be in at least a few of the Endicott cylinders.

We were standing in the open, two hundred feet from the nearest rocket launching pad, when we saw it—Littlefield's exploding star high up in the night sky. The brightness lasted less than ten seconds.


## CHAPTER TWENTY-ONE

YOU CAN BE HOLDING HIGH CARDS, practically unbeatable, in the final deal of a poker game and still not be sure of winning. You have to call your opponent's hand before he gets the idea that just by drawing out a gun and shooting you dead he can gather up all the chips, and cash them in by threatening further violence. Assuming, of course, that he's capable of that kind of violence and is in all respects the opposite of an honest gambler.

You can be even less sure of winning when it isn't a game of cards you're on the point of winning, but a duel to the death with a ruthless power combine and time is running out on you.

I had all the evidence I needed now to smash the Wendel Combine. But it had to be built up by legal experts, and stripped down as well, until the documentation had the sinewy, blockbusting persuasiveness of a champion's punch.

It would have to stir popular fury on Earth on a very wide scale, be made so convincing that no one could possibly mistake it for a trumped-up shakedown in another grab for power. And that would take time—two or three weeks, at least.

And right at the moment Wendel was almost certainly out of the hospital and back in the Wendel plant, getting ready to close in on the skyport with his army of goons.

The problem that confronted me can be summarized in just one sentence. I had to get into my uniform, pin the silver bird into place and complete just two visits, or Wendel would dig my grave wide and deep.

Not just my own grave, of course—but when you fight to stay alive you remember all of the things you want to protect and stay alive for. There are men, I suppose, who are chiefly concerned with survival on a more primitive plane, but I think I can honestly say I've never been that kind of man.

My first visit was going to be to one hell of a live man— Joseph Sherwood. Sherwood had undisputed custody, by authority of the Board, of every nuclear weapon in the Colony with enough large-scale destructive potential to make open defiance of that authority an extremely risky undertaking.

I was now his superior in rank, but I had no intention of making changes in his command or questioning the wisdom of the decisions he was more than qualified to make. The measures he had taken to protect the Colony I regarded as absolutely correct and he knew far more about nuclear armaments than I did. There were limits to what those measures could accomplish, because a large-scale thermonuclear weapon can destroy thousands of innocent victims, and the Wendel Combine knew precisely how far it could go without bringing down the thunder.

All I had to do was convince Wendel that it had now gone too far and that the thunder was very close. Basically it would be quite a simple undertaking. I would simply have to walk into the Wendel plant and talk to him in a calm way, at the risk of being blown apart.

I was standing before a full-length mirror in a small, windowless room, which the skyport officials had assured me, wasn't wired for sound. It sure had privacy. Not that I'd need it while I was putting on my uniform, because I'd be wearing it when I emerged and they would all see the silver bird. And Joan was the only woman in the building…which made privacy a little absurd on more than one count.

It was just that—well, when you stand before a mirror and pin that kind of insignia on a quite ordinary, regulation-fit uniform it does something to the wearer which changes the way he looks in a quite startling way.

I guess I just didn't want anyone to see me observing the change in a mirror and grin, which would have forced me to do something I just hadn't time for—take a sock at him. I suppose there's a little garden-variety vanity in me—show me a man who claims he hasn't a trace of it in his nature and I'll show you a first-class liar—but right at the moment I wouldn't have been lying if I'd said that nothing could have been further from my mind than preening myself on the way I looked.

But it was just as well I had privacy, because I had to stand before the mirror for three full minutes to get accustomed to the change, and feel relaxed and casual about it.

I'd forgotten to tell Commander Littlefield I'd be needing a tractor, warmed up and ready to roll, and that the place to find it waiting for me would be right outside the gate. The one I'd left there with a dead man sitting in it didn't have quite the trim, speedy look of three or four I'd noticed standing about the skyport and if he could get me a lighter one so much the better.

Joan was taking care of it for me. She came back just as I was turning from the mirror, with the silver bird gleaming on my right shoulder. She'd seen me wearing it before, of course, so she wasn't startled. But the tall, stoop-shouldered man with graying temples who had followed her into the room had enough startlement in his eyes to have made her a present of half of it and still made the grade in that respect.

He kept staring at the silver bird in tight-lipped silence until I darted a questioning glance at Joan and he seemed to realize he was putting a strain on my patience.

"My name's John Lynton," he said, hesitantly. "Commander Littlefield told me you'll be needing a tractor. I have one, and I'll be glad to drive you, sir. I brought the Endicott fuel cylinder to the skyport, so I naturally feel pretty strongly about everything that's happened. There's just one thing I'd like to see happen to Wendel. But I guess I don't have to spell it out for you, sir."

I stared at him in amazement. I'd taken it for granted that the Colonist who had delivered the cylinder was no longer at the skyport, because no one had pointed him out to me, and I'd been under too much of a strain to question Littlefield about it.

"Well...that takes care of one thing that puzzled me," I said. "I couldn't understand why you'd just deliver the cylinder and clear out. But people here seem to feel they're privileged to do pretty much as they please at times. So it didn't puzzle me too much."

"I was in the Administration Building, talking to a sky ship officer, when you were in the shed, sir," he explained. "But I saw you come into the projection room—"

"All right;" I said. "We haven't time to discuss it and it's not important anyway. I know how to drive a tractor, but I'm not an expert at it. If you've got your own tractor you'll know what to do if it breaks down. That's an advantage I'd be a fool to pass up. But if you're going with me, you may as well know we'll be in danger the instant we pass through the gate. The Wendel agents have orders to blast me down on sight."

I shouldn't have said that, for it made Joan bite down hard on her underlip and say in a kind of talking-to-herself whisper, "An armed escort would cut down the danger. Littlefield could—"

I shook my head. "We'd be certain to be stopped then and an open clash with Wendel agents in the streets of the Colony would wrap it up—but good. There's no way of packaging it that would please Wendel more."

The instant Lynton realized, just from the way I was looking at Joan, that I wanted to be alone with her he said: "I'd better check over the tractor once more. I'll drive it through the gate, draw in to the side of the clear-away and keep a sharp eye on the incoming traffic—if any. I'll keep the motor running, sir."

The instant the door closed behind him Joan was in my arms. For the most part all we did was embrace without saying a word, which is one way of saying as much as you possibly can in the space of half a minute.

I was a little afraid that Joan would break down and burst into tears, which would have spoiled everything. I could see the tears trembling on the fringes of her eyelids, and decided right then and there that she was one hell of a precious woman. And when you're parting with something very precious you can break your heart in two if you let yourself do too much thinking.

So I just kissed her very firmly on the mouth for the tenth time, swung about and walked out of that small, windowless room without looking back to see if she was still doing her best to keep the tears from flowing.

In the ambulance on the way to the hospital I'd seen more of the Colony than I could have covered on foot in half a day. Jogging through the streets again with Lynton doing the driving I could have taken in even more of it in a sightseeing way. I could have—but I didn't.

I saw no reason to make myself conspicuous, and somehow removing the insignia from my shoulder so soon after I'd pinned it on would have gone against the grain. And it wasn't just my uniform or the silver bird, which would have made me a sitting duck to a Wendel agent, stationed anywhere along the way with my description clear and sharp in his mind. It was a safe bet we'd pass at least a dozen of the Combine's goons, strutting about in their private police uniforms, so I took care to remain in a seated position in the back of the tractor, with my head well below sight-seeing level.

This time I didn't look, wonder or black out at intervals. I kept a tight grip on my nerves and refused to even let myself think what an impasse I'd be facing if my talk with Arms Custodian Sherwood didn't bring the kind of results I was counting on.

It's hard to maintain just one rigid mental stance when you're keeping a great many hard-to-control emotions bottled up in your mind with a clamped-down safety valve. But I didn't have to maintain the stance for long, because twenty minutes after we left the skyport the tractor rumbled to a halt before a massive, fortress-like building which stood a considerable distance from the buildings on both sides of it and was protected in its isolation by steel walls, pacing guards and a well-guarded stockpile of thermonuclear weapons.

No Wendel agent would have risked blasting away at me within three miles of that stronghold—unless he was tired of living and didn't want to see another Martian sunrise. It made me feel secure enough to stand up and descend from the tractor without making a production out of it, as if I was two-thirds convinced I'd be blown apart before I could advance twenty feet.

I neither hurried nor wasted time, just stood calmly by the tractor until I was satisfied no one who had seen us drive up—I was quite sure we were under long-range binocular scrutiny—would come striding out of the forest to question us at gunpoint. Then I nodded to Lynton, and walked straight toward the big gray building. I'd told him not to move from his seat until I came out, so there was no need to caution him further.

I can't remember at exactly what point in my approach to the high-walled gate the silver bird became a thunderbird, or exactly how each of the three guards looked when they first caught sight of it.

I was too startled just by the way the oldest of the three, who must have been a tow-headed twelve-year-old when the first wearer of the insignia walked the streets of the Colony, stared at me, snapped to attention and grounded the heavy weapon he'd been holding slantwise across his chest with a thud. The other two guards quickly followed suit. Quite possibly they had merely taken their cue from him and didn't want to risk an official reprimand. But they certainly put on a convincing performance, as if what they feared most was a full-dress court martial. If I'd dropped down out of the sky in a golden chariot and was Apollo, maybe, or the Aztec Sun God, I couldn't have been accorded more deference.

A moment later the high steel gate opened and shut with a clang and I was on the inside, with more guards on both sides of me. I'd paused a moment, of course, to explain to the elderly guard who had first saluted me, just why I was there and whom I wanted to see.

I had an escort of six guards as I walked to the end of the first-floor corridor, and ascended a short flight of stairs and they continued to escort all the way to the door of Sherwood's office.

Some men can be jolted almost speechless by an unexpected visit and recover their composure so rapidly they seem to have retained it from the beginning. It was that way with Sherwood. He was a big man in his early forties, with close-cropped reddish hair and handsome features.

He was sparing of words, but everything he told me was in direct answer to my questions and a man who can confine himself to just giving you the information you need without wasting words is likely to be the kind of man you can depend on in an emergency.

His final answer was the clincher. It came at the end of a fifteen-minute conversation.

"We can do it if we've no other choice," he said.

"All right," I said. "I want you to tell Wendel exactly what you've just told me, on a two-way televisual hookup. I'll be at the Wendel plant in fifteen minutes, and I'm sure I can persuade him to talk to you on the screen, right after I've laid it on the line for him.

"If," I added, "—and it's a very big *if*—I can get in to see him without ending up dead. His goons have orders to blast me down on sight."

He looked at me steadily for a moment, with a concerned tightening of his lips. Then he leaned back and some of the strain left his face.

"Have any of his goons ever seen you with that insignia on your shoulder?" he asked.

It was a good question and it confirmed the opinion I'd formed of him.

"No, they haven't," I said. "But it doesn't alter the possibility I'll be blasted down before I can get in to see Wendel. Remember—the Wendel Combine has taken the big gamble and is waging an undeclared, but all out war. This insignia makes me Target Number One. If I took it off before entering the plant his goons would probably recognize me anyway—too quickly for me to save myself by shouting at them and trying to make them see that Wendel would want them to withhold their fire. I may not have a chance to do any explaining, because they may recognize me just from the description that's been furnished them."

Sherwood nodded. "Yes…it would be foolish to deny you won't be exposing yourself to danger. And you'll have to be wearing the insignia when you confront Wendel. But I've a feeling that Wendel's goons will take you straight to him. I could be mistaken, of course. But somehow I can't picture them firing pointblank at Target Number One without prior authorization. They'd be sticking out their necks with a vengeance, because their instructions to blast you on sight were issued before you pinned that bird on your shoulder."

"I hope you're right," I said. "But goons are funny people."

"I'll be right here at my desk when the screen lights up," he said. "Don't worry too much. I'll handle my end of it with very careful timing…"

Fifteen minutes later my tractor rumbled to a halt for the second time, directly in front of the Wendel plant.

Like the Endicott plant, it faced a big square and there were no pedestrians in sight on the side we parked on.

"This time I'm going with you," Lynton said, very firmly.

So he was going with me! All right, it was an obligation I owed him, and I couldn't pull rank on him, because he was a civilian and it wouldn't have done the least bit of good.

Moreover, he'd gotten over being dazzled by the silver bird, if it had ever really dazzled him, which I doubted. He was a too tough-fibered, independent, non-authority conscious kind of guy. You find them in every rugged, pioneering society guys who will stand up in a public meeting and tell a governmental big shot that the speech he's just delivered has a phony ring to it and he'd be well advised to try again.

I descended from the tractor a little more cautiously this time, keeping my eye on the ground-floor windows of the plant and wondering how long it would take me to cross from the car to the building's wide main entrance and if the steel-mesh blinds on the windows might not be a cover-up for nuclear weapons pointed straight in our direction.

But actually, despite the uneasiness, which we both felt, we crossed from the tractor to the plant without hurrying and with our shoulders held straight.

There were two guards in Wendel private police uniforms with nuclear handguns clamped to their hips standing just inside the entrance and the instant we came into view their hands darted to the holstered weapons and their eyes took on a steely glint.

Then—both guards did a swift double take. They didn't stiffen to attention the way the guards at the gate of the nuclear fortress had done, but something happened to their faces, which made them seem to be wearing frozen masks. Only their eyes remained alive, alert, the steely glint replaced by a look of stunned incredulity.

I spoke sharply, without giving them time to reach a decision on their own initiative which might have had tragic consequences, for you can never tell what desperate, completely unjustified measures a badly jolted man will take it into his head to resort to.

"I'm here to see Wendel," I said. "Nobody else will do. I guess I don't have to tell you that this is an order. You'd be very foolish not to unbar that gate, for I have the authority to take you into custody if you prevent me from entering the plant. You may be just guards, but that will not prevent the Colonization Board from imprisoning you on a treason charge."

Their eyes never left the insignia while they were swinging open the big, iron-barred entrance gate for me. It was set well back from the street, with enough walled-in space in front of it to accommodate a dozen bloody corpses. I had an idea they would have tried to make use of it in that way, if I'd attempted to force my way past them with an armed escort and hadn't been wearing the silver bird.

The strain and uncertainty eased a little once we were fairly sure we wouldn't be blasted down without warning. It didn't take long for that near-assurance to harden into a conviction, for what happened after the big gate clanged shut behind us was almost a repeat of what had taken place in the nuclear fortress.

More armed Wendel police guards fell into step on both sides of us, with much the same look on their faces the two at the entrance had worn ten seconds after their eyes had rested on the silver bird.

Just one small incident took place, which made it a little unlike the reception that had been accorded me when I'd asked to see Sherwood. We were held up at the end of a branching corridor while one of the guards went into a small, blank-walled room and buzzed Wendel on an interplant communicator, announcing our arrival.

We didn't know that until later, because he was careful to shut the door of the room before he spoke into the communicator. When he came out there was a hardness around his eyes, a look of grim satisfaction that should have warned me that we were in danger. But you don't always attach as much weight as you should to a quick change of expression on the face of a man whose job requires him to resort to brutal violence two or three times a week. The face of such a man can harden just from habit.

Because it was the kind of mistake it was easy to make and the other guards were keeping their hostility under wraps we didn't know or even suspect that we were walking straight into a trap until we were almost at the door of Wendel's office on the second floor of the plant.

If you're the head of a big power combine, and shrewd, as Wendel unquestionably was, and there's a threat to your survival coming straight toward you along an echoing corridor and you want to be sure in advance he'll be a broken man when you talk with him in strict privacy, with the chips scattered widely and the game almost at an end—you'll either take care of it yourself, or assign just one man you can trust to do the job for you.

Not a dozen men—or half a dozen—but just one. It's more efficient that way, more certain, the right way to go about it.

I had no way of knowing that, of course, no way of looking through a wall at Wendel standing motionless or possibly seated in a chair, his eyes gleaming triumphantly, as we approached the door of his office, with just one guard walking a few paces behind us.

Except that—deep in my mind the alarm bells were ringing again. They were ringing, all right, but very, very faintly and I don't know to this day what made me turn my head and look behind me just as he was whipping out the heavy metal thong.

I caught only the barest glimpse of the thong gleaming in the corridor light. But even if he'd kept it concealed for a few seconds longer his face would have given him away. His eyes were blazing with a savage enmity, and he started for me the instant he realized that I had been forewarned.

I gripped Lynton by the arm and fell back against the wall, tugging him around so that he was far enough behind me to give me a chance to grapple with Hard Eyes head-on, with complete freedom of movement.

He made the mistake of coming at me too fast. It might not have been a mistake if he hadn't been so reckless with the thong, trying to lash me across the chest with it before he was sure of his balance. The sheer weight of the weapon carried him forward, straight past me, and it went swishing through the air without hitting anything.

I made a grab for his wrist and before he could recover his balance I was twisting it relentlessly and slamming my fist against the side of his head. He sank to his knees and I kept right on hammering away at him, hitting him first on the right temple and then on the left and not even stopping to take the thong away from him.

There was no need for me to relieve him of the thong, for he flattened out on the floor still holding on to it and passed out cold. It seemed only reasonable and just to let him keep it as a souvenir.

I was out of breath and feeling a little dizzy, because when you hit anyone as hard as I'd hit Hard Eyes, not caring much whether I killed him or not, it takes a minute or two to recover. I still hadn't quite gotten my breath back when the door of Wendel's office slammed open and Wendel himself stood there, staring down at the guard with a look of consternation on his face.

I became a little alarmed when I saw that Lynton had moved out from the wall and was making straight for him with his arm drawn back. Hell—that's an understatement. I became very much alarmed, because the one thing I didn't want was to have Wendel belted unconscious and laid out on the floor at the guard's side before I could have a talk with him.

I got between them just in time, and I grabbed Wendel by the shoulders and hurled him back into his office and when he staggered a little and almost fell I grabbed hold of him for the second time, and slammed him down in the chair in front of his big, metal-topped desk.

He looked up at me for a moment with a killing rage in his eyes, but I didn't give him a chance to get his breath back. For the barest instant, though, if he had been quick enough, he might have succeeded in getting to his feet and lashing out at me, for I saw something on the opposite side of the room that seemed almost too good to be true, and I took three full seconds out to stare at it.

It was a big tele-communicator screen—just the kind of screen I had been sure I'd find somewhere in the plant, but hardly in Wendel's private office. The fact that Sherwood had one in his office was not quite so surprising, for Sherwood's custodianship of thermonuclear weapons had made him more communication-conscious.

I'd counted on being able to persuade Wendel to accompany me to wherever the plant's screen happened to be located, after I'd had a serious talk with him. But since he hadn't wanted me to have a talk with him until he'd done his best to get me killed or crippled for life, and I would now have to keep him boxed up in his office by force while we conducted the talk, having the screen so accessible was one hell of a lucky break.

"Shut the door," I told Lynton. "And lock it."

I waited until Lynton had complied, my hands on Wendel's shoulders with so fierce a clamp-hold that he gave up trying to rise.

"You'll never get out of here alive!" he choked. "If you think—"

"Don't press your luck, Wendel," I said, warningly. "I might be tempted to break your neck."

"That insignia you're wearing doesn't mean a thing now, Graham. Don't you understand? You couldn't command a fly to crawl over a bread crumb. The Wendel Combine is taking over the Colony."

"Not a fly, Wendel," I said. "The Wendel Combine. A big boa constrictor has nothing in common with a fly and I'm not interested in bread crumbs. And this will surprise you. *You're* going to do the commanding. You're going to command the boa constrictor to start disgorging—every kill it's ever swallowed. It's going to flatten itself out until it's just a mass of cold mottled skin, which the Board will know how to deal with."

"Who's going to make me?"

"I am," I said. "You have just ten minutes to make up your mind. You either turn over all of the Combine's nuclear weapons to the Board, break the back of the Wendel police force by arresting all of its officers and placing yourself under house arrest and order every Wendel employee to cooperate with the Board or—Joseph Sherwood will vaporize the plant with a thermonuclear bomb. The rocket will be guided by remote control and will hover directly above the plant until the bomb has been dropped. Only the plant will be destroyed. There will be no zone of spreading radioactive contamination."

All of the color drained from Wendel's face, leaving it ashen. "You must be mad!" he gasped. "You'd die too."

"I'm aware of that," I said. "We'll all be vaporized together. But it isn't too bad a way to die, Wendel. You feel no pain, never know—"

"Do you expect me to take that threat seriously?" he breathed.

"I'm afraid I do," I said. I gestured toward the tele-communicator. "Sherwood will tell you how serious it is. He's waiting to talk to you. Suppose we turn that screen on and listen to what he has to say. I'm sure you know how to get the right wavelength. The Wendel spy network would hardly fail to keep you informed when Sherwood changes the code frequencies."

"You said ten minutes," Wendel was breathing harshly now and the veins on his forehead were thick blue cords. "You'd have to let Sherwood know when to drop the bomb. You haven't been in communication with him since you arrived here. Suppose I refuse to dial? That's a very intricate, highly specialized communicator. You couldn't operate it."

That made me change my mind about letting him do the dialing. I was pretty sure I'd experience no difficulty in getting in contact with Sherwood and I didn't want to give Wendel a chance to make the communicator even more specialized by ripping out some of the wiring.

I turned to Lynton and indicated by tapping Wendel forcibly on the shoulder that I was about to relinquish my hold on the Combine's difficult president, and would he kindly take my place behind the chair.

"Don't let him move," I cautioned, when we'd changed places. "Keep a tight grip on his shoulders."

"Don't worry," Lynton said. "If he moves an inch I'll do what you said might not be a bad idea—break his neck."

It didn't take me long to discover that Wendel had lied about the communicator, which meant, of course, that he had been hoping I'd give him a chance to do a quick job of sabotage on the wiring.

It was just a run-of-the-mill, two-way televisual communicator, with nothing specialized about it.

There was a humming sound for a few seconds right after I'd finished dialing and it gave me a chance to scrutinize Wendel's face to see how he was taking it.

He was terrified, all right. But his lips were still set in defiant lines and I was sure that if he could have gotten a grip on my throat right at that moment getting his fingers unlocked wouldn't have been easy.

I thought that when Sherwood's image appeared on the screen there would be just one minute of hard-to-live-through uncertainty—that he'd back up what I'd told Wendel with his hand on the rocket release button and look straight at me, as if awaiting a signal I had no intention of giving.

But I suddenly realized I didn't know just how it was going to be. Would Wendel stay defiant right up to the end, would he defeat me through sheer stubbornness, even though he was mortally terrified?

But there was one thing I did know. For the first time, as I waited for Sherwood's image to appear on the screen, I knew with absolute certainty, beyond any possibility of doubt that I could never go through with it.

The rocket had to be prepared and ready—the nuclear deterrent had to be a reality—or I could never have carried the bluff through with the kind of confidence that just the knowledge that you're holding the highest cards in the deck can give you.

I had to feel that I *just might give the signal.*

But vaporizing the plant would have cost the lives of thirty thousand people and not more than a fourth of them were vicious criminals. I just couldn't see myself ordering a nuclear bomb to be dropped on more than twenty thousand completely innocent Wendel plant engineers and laboratory technicians.

Perhaps I shouldn't have felt that way, because if the Wendel Combine took over the Colony three or four times that number of innocent people would perish, or sink into degradation and become completely enslaved. But I did feel that way and—well, I wouldn't have to live with what I'd done, because I'd be killed by the blast. But I didn't want that on my conscience even as a dead man.

I couldn't go through with it, but had I ever really intended to? It didn't mean I couldn't win, didn't change what I'd come to do. If I could carry my bluff through without flinching, right up to the zero-count instant, there was a very good chance that Wendel would crack. A very good chance still.

I had the highest cards in the deck and was only handicapped in one way. If the zero-count instant came and Wendel didn't crack I couldn't play them.

I've never really believed in miracles. But if you're holding what you think are the highest cards, and something happens to your hand you never dreamed could happen—if you look and see you've got a card that's even higher, just slipped in between the others as a gift...well, that's pretty close to a miracle, isn't it?

I thought when Sherwood's image appeared on the screen he'd be sitting alone behind his desk, with his thumb on the rocket-release button. But he wasn't alone and when I saw who was with him I almost stopped breathing...

Joan was with him and she was looking straight at me out of the screen.

"Don't do it, Ralph!" she pleaded. "Oh, God, no—"

Then I saw that she was staring past me and without turning I knew that she was appealing to Wendel with the same look of pleading desperation in her eyes. "If he gives the signal his command will be obeyed. And he'll do it unless you stop him! When you've lived with a man in the intimacy of marriage—yes, that's important and I have to say it—you know him better than anyone else. You know what he's capable of. He'll give the signal unless you do as he says, because the insignia he's wearing gives him no choice. If you don't stop him now... *you'll die with him!*"

I turned then and stared straight at Wendel. I'd never seen a man sag before in quite the way he did. All of the life seemed to go out of his eyes. His defiance gave way to a look of utter hopelessness, of abject surrender, and he sank so low in his chair that he seemed on the verge of slumping to the floor, despite Lynton's grip on his shoulders.

His voice, when he spoke, scarcely rose above a whisper. "All right, Graham," he said. "You win."

As I turned back to the screen and saw the look of overwhelming relief and gratefulness in Joan's eyes I couldn't help wondering how close she had been to being right. Had the insignia really given me any choice? If Wendel had stayed defiant and refused to crack—would I have gone through with it? How much does any man know about *himself*?

I'd probably never know the answer.

In the days that followed every one of the Wendel agents were rounded up and returned to Earth to stand trial. I never did find out the identity of the agent who had shot the dart at me from high up on the spiral or the one who had sent a little mechanical killer in my direction by the shores of Lake Michigan in New Chicago.

It didn't worry me at all, because I was sure that both of those delightful characters were among the agents who had been rounded up in the mopping up operations.

Oh, yes—they rescued her with her hair in disarray and no longer standing high up on her head. Three days later, drifting through empty space about three hundred thousand miles from Mars. She's in prison now and will have to answer charges. But I intend to go all out in the plea I'll make in her defense when she comes up for trial.

Some judges are enlightened and merciful and others are harsh tyrants, but with the backing of the Board I'm not too worried about the outcome. If it goes against us, I'll take it to the highest court in the land, and the backing of the Board carries plenty of weight there too.

Eventually I forgave Commander Littlefield.

"I'm a hard man, Ralph," he said, standing in the starlight outside the Port Administration Section with a crumpled sheet of paper in his hand, right after he'd received assurances from Earth he'd be placed in command of a new sky ship. "I did what I did because I am what I am. I knew that her life hung in the balance, that every word we exchanged increased the danger. But when I weighed that against the future of the Colony—I felt I had no choice. I knew what a full confession would mean to us."

I never saw Nurse Cherubin again. She married her doctor and they were honeymoon passengers on the next scheduled Earth trip, which took place while I was busy making sure that the whole Wendel Combine would come apart at the seams. It was a little like watching a volcanic explosion and keeping the lava flow channeled with the full weight of the Board's authority.

Joan and I have become Martian Colony residents for the duration. I mean by that there will always be new battles to be fought in a war that will never end…as long as Man stays a part of the universe. There's something embattled about him that you don't find in any other species. Maybe it's good and maybe it's bad, but it helps to explain why he keeps building for the future. He never knows—and just not knowing makes him want to build as sturdily as he can.

You never prize anything so much as when you feel you're about to lose it. So you fight to preserve it, and when you've done that you've built up enough excess energy to want to make a stab at something better. And when that's threatened you'll fight again and so on until the final curtain.

It's just the way things are.


## THE END

*If you've enjoyed this book, you will not want to miss these terrific titles…*

## ARMCHAIR SCI-FI, FANTASY, & HORROR DOUBLE NOVELS, $12.95 *each*

**D-1**   **THE GALAXY RAIDERS** by William P. McGivern
**SPACE STATION #1** by Frank Belknap Long

**D-2**   **THE PROGRAMMED PEOPLE** by Jack Sharkey
**SLAVES OF THE CRYSTAL BRAIN** by William Carter Sawtelle

**D-3**   **YOU'RE ALL ALONE** by Fritz Leiber
**THE LIQUID MAN** by Bernard C. Gilford

**D-4**   **CITADEL OF THE STAR LORDS** by Edmund Hamilton
**VOYAGE TO ETERNITY** by Milton Lesser

**D-5**   **IRON MEN OF VENUS** by Don Wilcox
**THE MAN WITH ABSOLUTE MOTION** by Noel Loomis

**D-6**   **WHO SOWS THE WIND...** by Rog Phillips
**THE PUZZLE PLANET** by Robert A. W. Lowndes

**D-7**   **PLANET OF DREAD** by Murray Leinster
**TWICE UPON A TIME** by Charles L. Fontenay

**D-8**   **THE TERROR OUT OF SPACE** by Dwight V. Swain
**QUEST OF THE GOLDEN APE** by Ivar Jorgensen and Adam Chase

**D-9**   **SECRET OF MARRACOTT DEEP** by Henry Slesar
**PAWN OF THE BLACK FLEET** by Mark Clifton.

**D-10**   **BEYOND THE RINGS OF SATURN** by Robert Moore Williams
**A MAN OBSESSED** by Alan E. Nourse

## ARMCHAIR SCIENCE FICTION CLASSICS, $12.95 each

**C-1**   **THE GREEN MAN**
by Harold M. Sherman

**C-2**   **A TRACE OF MEMORY**
By Keith Laumer

**C-3**   **INTO PLUTONIAN DEPTHS**
by Stanton A. Coblentz

## ARMCHAIR MASTERS OF SCIENCE FICTION SERIES, $16.95 each

**M-1**   **MASTERS OF SCIENCE FICTION, Vol. One**
Bryce Walton—"Dark of the Moon" and other tales

**M-2**   **MASTERS OF SCIENCE FICTION, Vol. Two**
Jerome Bixby: "One Way Street" and other tales

*If you've enjoyed this book, you will not want to miss these terrific titles…*

## ARMCHAIR SCI-FI & HORROR DOUBLE NOVELS, $12.95 each

**D-11**　**PERIL OF THE STARMEN** by Kris Neville
**THE STRANGE INVASION** by Murray Leinster

**D-12**　**THE STAR LORD** by Boyd Ellanby
**CAPTIVES OF THE FLAME** by Samuel R. Delaney

**D-13**　**MEN OF THE MORNING STAR** by Edmund Hamilton
**PLANET FOR PLUNDER** by Hal Clement and Sam Merwin, Jr.

**D-14**　**ICE CITY OF THE GORGON** by Chester S. Geier and Richard Shaver
**WHEN THE WORLD TOTTERED** by Lester Del Rey

**D-15**　**WORLDS WITHOUT END** by Clifford D. Simak
**THE LAVENDER VINE OF DEATH** by Don Wilcox

**D-16**　**SHADOW ON THE MOON** by Joe Gibson
**ARMAGEDDON EARTH** by Geoff St. Reynard

**D-17**　**THE GIRL WHO LOVED DEATH** by Paul W. Fairman
**SLAVE PLANET** by Laurence M. Janifer

**D-18**　**SECOND CHANCE** by J. F. Bone
**MISSION TO A DISTANT STAR** by Frank Belknap Long

**D-19**　**THE SYNDIC** by C. M. Kornbluth
**FLIGHT TO FOREVER** by Poul Anderson

**D-20**　**SOMEWHERE I'LL FIND YOU** by Milton Lesser
**THE TIME ARMADA** by Fox B. Holden

## ARMCHAIR SCIENCE FICTION CLASSICS, $12.95 each

**C-4**　**CORPUS EARTHLING**
by Louis Charbonneau

**C-5**　**THE TIME DISSOLVER**
by Jerry Sohl

**C-6**　**WEST OF THE SUN**
by Edgar Pangborn

## ARMCHAIR SCIENCE FICTION & HORROR GEMS SERIES, $12.95 each

**G-1**　**SCIENCE FICTION GEMS, Vol. One**
Isaac Asimov and others

**G-2**　**HORROR GEMS, Vol. One**
Carl Jacobi and others

*If you've enjoyed this book, you will not want to miss these terrific titles…*

## ARMCHAIR SCI-FI, FANTASY, & HORROR DOUBLE NOVELS, $12.95 each

**D-21**   **EMPIRE OF EVIL** by Robert Arnette
**THE SIGN OF THE TIGER** by Alan E. Nourse & J. A. Meyer

**D-22**   **OPERATION SQUARE PEG** by Frank Belknap Long
**ENCHANTRESS OF VENUS** by Leigh Brackett

**D-23**   **THE LIFE WATCH** by Lester Del Rey
**CREATURES OF THE ABYSS** by Murray Leinster

**D-24**   **LEGION OF LAZARUS** by Edmond Hamilton
**STAR HUNTER** by Andre Norton

**D-25**   **EMPIRE OF WOMEN** by John Fletcher
**ONE OF OUR CITIES IS MISSING** by Irving Cox

**D-26**   **THE WRONG SIDE OF PARADISE** by Raymond F. Jones
**THE INVOLUNTARY IMMORTALS** by Rog Phillips

**D-27**   **EARTH QUARTER** by Damon Knight
**ENVOY TO NEW WORLDS** by Keith Laumer

**D-28**   **SLAVES TO THE METAL HORDE** by Milton Lesser
**HUNTERS OUT OF TIME** by Joseph E. Kelleam

**D-29**   **RX JUPITER SAVE US** by Ward Moore
**BEWARE THE USURPERS** by Geoff St. Reynard

**D-30**   **SECRET OF THE SERPENT** by Don Wilcox
**CRUSADE ACROSS THE VOID** by Dwight V. Swain

## ARMCHAIR SCIENCE FICTION CLASSICS, $12.95 each

**C-7**   **THE SHAVER MYSTERY, pt. 1**
by Richard S. Shaver

**C-8**   **THE SHAVER MYSTERY, pt. 2**
by Richard S. Shaver

**C-9**   **MURDER IN SPACE** by David V. Reed
by David V. Reed

## ARMCHAIR MASTERS OF SCIENCE FICTION SERIES, $16.95 each

**M-3**   **MASTERS OF SCIENCE FICTION, Vol. Three**
Robert Sheckley

**M-4**   **MASTERS OF SCIENCE FICTION, Vol. Four**
Mack Reynolds, part one

*If you've enjoyed this book, you will not want to miss these terrific titles…*

## ARMCHAIR SCI-FI & HORROR DOUBLE NOVELS, $12.95 each

**D-31**   **A HOAX IN TIME** by Keith Laumer
**INSIDE EARTH** by Poul Anderson

**D-32**   **TERROR STATION** by Dwight V. Swain
**THE WEAPON FROM ETERNITY** by Dwight V. Swain

**D-33**   **THE SHIP FROM INFINITY** by Edmond Hamilton
**TAKEOFF** by C. M. Kornbluth

**D-34**   **THE METAL DOOM** by David H. Keller
**TWELVE TIMES ZERO** by Howard Browne

**D-35**   **HUNTERS OUT OF SPACE** by Joseph Kelleam
**INVASION FROM THE DEEP** by Paul W. Fairman,

**D-36**   **THE BEES OF DEATH** by Robert Moore Williams
**A PLAGUE OF PYTHONS** by Frederick Pohl

**D-37**   **THE LORDS OF QUARMALL** by Fritz Leiber and Harry Fischer
**BEACON TO ELSEWHERE** by James H. Schmitz

**D-38**   **BEYOND PLUTO** by John S. Campbell
**ARTERY OF FIRE** by Thomas N. Scortia

**D-39**   **SPECIAL DELIVERY** by Kris Neville
**NO TIME FOR TOFFEE** by Charles F. Meyers

**D-40**   **JUNGLE IN THE SKY** by Milton Lesser
**RECALLED TO LIFE** by Robert Silverberg

## ARMCHAIR SCIENCE FICTION CLASSICS, $12.95 each

**C-10**   **MARS IS MY DESTINATION**
by Frank Belknap Long

**C-11**   **SPACE PLAGUE**
by George O. Smith

**C-12**   **SO SHALL YE REAP**
by Rog Phillips

## ARMCHAIR SCIENCE FICTION & HORROR GEMS SERIES, $12.95 each

**G-3**   **SCIENCE FICTION GEMS, Vol. Two**
James Blish and others

**G-4**   **HORROR GEMS, Vol. Two**
Joseph Payne Brennan and others